CACHINNATION

NOVEMBER

WILLIAM LEROY

ISBN 979-8-9869494-8-2

$7.99

50799>

9 798986 949482

Mossik Press

CACHINNATION

NOVEMBER

WILLIAM LEROY

We don't laugh because we're happy.

We're happy because we laugh.

Jewish Proverb

WEDNESDAY

November 19, 2025

CHAPTER ONE

Ha, ha, ha, ha, ha, ha, ha, ha...

Perched on a stool at the Wide-O-Wake Cafe counter for his usual mid-morning snack — today, pancakes wreathed in link sausages — Max tried to block out annoying racket coming from a corner table of other coffee-break regulars:

Leo Wolfe, a traveling salesman, recently returned to town and now working as an armed security guard at his brother-in-law's Main Street pawn shop.

Harry "Scratchy" Katz, owner of the Oldies-'n'-Goodies used furniture-and-antiques store.

Dan "Possum" McGill, a veterinarian and taxidermist.

Bill "Rabbit" Roberts, a town hall clerk who...

"Damn thing was stuck so tight I thought I'd never get it out," Wiley "Coyote" Johnson, a handyman, was now loudly shop-talking.

"That's what she said," Leo Wolfe bellowed.

Ha, Ha, ha, ha, ha, ha, ha...

Max knew them all, slightly, though not by their in-group nicknames that he'd overheard. Collectively they called themselves the "Furries" and seemed to always be having more fun than a barrel of monkeys.

"So I said, 'don't eat that, lady, it's horseshit.'"

Ha, ha, ha, ha, ha, ha, ha...

"That was no lady. That was my wife!"

Ha, ha, ha, ha, ha, ha, ha...

Max was envious. As a former long-term member of the U.S. Postal Service, he'd spent many a happy hour hanging out with buddies in the post office Rubber Room...relieving stress... shooting breeze... and...

"...so the farmer's daughter said to the traveling salesman, 'That's not a cow, and you're not milking it!'"

Ha, ha, ha, ha, ha, ha, ha...

"And the farmer's wife said, "Don't sell that cow!" Ha, ha, ha..."

"Different joke, Possum, and needs to be told right. Try to keep up."

"Any of you boys want another round before I wash out the pot?" Charlie, the counter man yelled.

"That's what she said," Leo Wolfe yelled back.

Ha, ha, ha, ha, ha, ha, ha...

There was always an empty chair at the corner table, but...

"Caught his wife in bed with his best friend, and said, "For cryin' out loud, Joe, I have to do it, but you...?""

Ha, ha, ha, ha, ha, ha, ha...

Max had never been invited to have a seat at the table of "Furries" and didn't dare...Not that he still minded getting blackballed by the Veterans of Foreign Wars Auxiliary. Heck, most Auxiliary members were broads and, as only the son of a veteran with no actual war stories to tell, he would have felt out of place.

"Hand this over to the boys, would ya, Maxie," said Charlie, putting a pot of coffee on the counter. "But careful, it's hot."

"That's what she said."

Ha, ha, ha, ha, ha, ha, ha...

"Put it there, Max," said "Possum" McGill. "Wolfie's just leaving."

"That's what she said."

Ha, ha, ha, ha, ha, ha, ha...

"Yeah, have a seat in the laughing place, Br'er Bear," said Wolfe, rising from his chair. "But don't look at me. I'm not the only one around here who starts forest fires."

Ha, ha, ha, ha, ha, ha, ha...

"Yeah, tell us, Bear: When you poop in the woods, does anybody hear you? Ha, ha..."

"Again, not funny, Possum," said Wolfe, before announcing he had an appointment, was in a "wildcattin'" mood, and was going to have a dentist drill at random.

Ha, ha, ha, ha, ha, ha, ha, ha...

"Always leave 'em laughing. Ha, ha, ha..."

"Good, he's gone," McGill then semi-whispered, "and doesn't suspect a thing. Tonight we get the last laugh at the Big Bad Wolfe's comeuppance."

Hmmm.

Max was ticked pink, so to speak, to be a Furry, to have a nickname for the first time in his life, and to be included in the "payback" plotted by his new pals in return for jokes played on them by their old pal, Leo Wolfe, but...

Hmmm.

"Br'er Bear", he recalled, was the moniker for the dumb storybook character who didn't get the punchlines of jokes, and walked into a hornets nest after being lured by B'rer Rabbit to a so-called "laughing place".

CHAPTER TWO

♫*Will you make me happy for the rest of my life?/Will you take me away and make me your wife?...* ♫

With an old song inside her head flooding her mind with bitter memories, Lil McGill sat at a cafe table for one... still pretending to read an article in the magazine she'd propped open to avoid being seen by Leo Wolfe...still thinking of herself as the pathetic middle-aged "Lorraine McFly" in *Back to the Future*... and still seething.

Ha, ha, ha, ha, ha...

Across the room, her so-called husband, "Possum", continued to yuk it up with other losers, though among his many deficiencies was absence of a reliable funny bone.

♫*When the feeling came over me like a tidal wave/ I started swearing to God and on my mother's grave/ I swore that I would love you 'til the end of time...* ♫

Leo was a classic Alpha-dog, and a boyfriend in her distant teenaged past. He'd called her "Beaver" and her almost equally embarrassing adolescent nickname for him had been...Anyway, everyone, including herself, had expected that they—King and Queen of the Senior Prom—would get married after graduation, but...

"That's what you get for not putting out," her clueless sister had said when Leo and she broke up.

Ha, ha, ha, ha, ha...

Lil put down the magazine, discreetly took a flask from a tote, and added a few drops of "courage" to her bitter cup.

They'd had a spat. Leo took out his frustration on Possum.

She had felt sorry for the young "George McFly", a mousy nerd with yellowish rodent-like teeth, but already enrolled in college with plans to become a doctor and…Okay, like a pathetic teenaged "Lorraine McFly", she had wanted to make Leo, the local version of "Biff Tannen", jealous…

♫ *So now I'm praying for the end of time to arrive/ 'Cause if I gotta spend another minute with you I don't think I can survive…* ♫

Ha, ha, ha, ha, ha…

She married Possum. Leo left town. Seven months later, little Leon was born. And for almost thirty long, boring years since then…

Ha, ha, ha, ha, ha…

Now the prom king was back in town, taking time off from a successful business career to help his brother-in-law at the Hock 'Em Up pawn shop. Still rosy-cheeked. Still sporting a thick mane of curly red hair. Still the center of attention. Still…

"You remember Max Morgan," said Possum, suddenly standing at her table beside a semi-familiar overweight man wearing an old-fashioned double-breasted suit, tie, and felt hat. "Max is a Notary Public, and Leo just made him a Furry. Probably to set up a line of fat jokes. Yuk, yuk, yuk."

"Yeah, Yours Truly is a stamper, but also mainly a private dick," said the newest butt of Leo's jokes. "And as a matter of fact, Brad Runyon a/k/a the Fat Man back in the *Noir* is my role model. Overweight, yeah, but quick on his feet, and a good dancer. A natty dresser, and…"

"When the doctor stripped him down and told him to diet, Max asked, what color? Yuk, yuk, yuk. And that was what she said! Yuk, yuk, yuk."

As the fat man waddled toward the cafe counter…"Did you catch Leo's eye on his way out?" her so-called husband semi-whispered. "Did he take the bait?"

Lil drained her cup. She had tentatively given in to Possum's nagging, but…

"Leo used to think you were hot, yuk, yuk, yuk," her hopeless husband had said earlier, which was doubly insulting. And now that she'd had second thoughts, along with an ounce or two of "courage"…

"No!" Lil declared. "I did not 'catch his eye'. I will not be pimped!"

"Aw, it's just a joke, Lil. Heck, I have to do it, but not Leo. Yuk, yuk, yuk…"

♫♪*I'm praying for the end of time, it's all that I can do/ Praying for the end of time, so I can end my time with you*♫♪

CHAPTER THREE

"Haw, haw, haw…"

"No, no, no, you're braying," said Frances Quinzel, a middle-aged broad seated across from Max inside her out-of-town clinic."Try again."

"Ho, ho, ho…"

"No, no, no, not unless coupled with the telling or hearing of a Santa joke during the jolly Christmas season. Try again."

"Hee, hee, hee…"

"Disdainful, Mr. Morgan. A smarty-pants giggle that implies condescension. Try to be mirthful."

"Heh, heh, heh…"

"A chortle? You call that mirthful? Kin to a cackle — suggestive of mild amusement perhaps — but often as not implying evil intent if not actual plotting."

His normal "ha, ha, ha" had also failed to achieve the hilarity of what Ms. Quinzel described as "cachinnation". And dang it, while the broad recommended by Possum McGill may have researched the practices of hyenas — and might be a laughter expert as reputed — she seemed not to realize that fat guys were not necessarily jolly, especially during the lead-up to Christmas.

Yours truly had never been much of an LOLer at any time of year, and since becoming a hardboiled private dick…

"You more so than others should understand that the soul of both pathos and humor is the same…"

Pathos?

"Reactions to both tragedy and comedy are based on a sense of things being not what they ought to be. As revealed by an unexpected punchline to a joke, much like what you might call a 'switcheroo' in one of your investigations."

Switcheroos in Yours Truly's investigations were never funny, but...

"Yes, the Theory of Incongruity is the most commonly accepted explanation of humor. When a joke begins, our minds and bodies anticipate what's going to happen and how it will end. Funny happens when another outcome occurs. In other words, when things are "out of whack", as Dr. Seuss put it."

Max sighed. By Seuss' definition, his whole life was a joke, but...

"The Theory of Relief, properly understood, is complementary to the Theory of Incongruity," the bookish expert continued. "Physically, laughter involves contraction of fifteen facial muscles. Half-closing of the larynx upsets the respiratory system, causing irregular air intake. Tear ducts are sometimes activated, so while the mouth is opening and closing in a continuing struggle for oxygen, the face becomes moist, often red or even purple.

"Indeed, it's not uncommon for people to actually die laughing, due to a ruptured brain aneurism...collapsed lung...strangulated hernia...gelastic seizures...asphyxiation...cardiac arrest..."

Max began to feel better about his inability to yuk, a condition the vet had diagnosed as something called "gelophobia", meaning fear of laughing and/or being laughed at.

"But usually, vocalization of the physical and mental reactions to humor—which is to say, laughter—provides a beneficial relief of tension. Said by some to have originated in humans as expressions of shared relief from the passing of danger, resulting relaxation that inhibits the fight-or-flight response is conducive to bonding with others. No sane person laughs out loud while alone, but in comfortable company with others, cachinnation is infectious.

"As the trite saying goes: 'Laugh, and the world laughs with you. Cry, and you cry alone.'"

Uh oh, just as he feared: unless and until he got over his case of gelophobia—or maybe brought along a canister of laughing gas—he would not fit in with the jovial Furries at tonight's scheduled get-together.

Speaking of which—as the brainy broad rattled on about laughing at jokes as surrender to recognition and reconciliation with a "butt's" own foolish "foibles"—Max looked at his watch.

Due to road construction, the twenty-mile drive to the county seat town of Okmulgee had taken almost an hour. His laughing lessons had already consumed almost another hour. And he still had to pick up a suitable outfit for tonight's surprise party for Leo Wolfe.

"...all about bullies establishing a sense of dominance, according to the Superiority Theory," the wordy teacher was saying. "As I have repeatedly advised Mr. McGill, when confronted by someone 'making fun' of another, even if amused, ask yourself: If that bully—a Mr. Wolfe he always talks about—told a joke while alone in the woods, would it be funny? In other words, it takes two to tango. So never laugh at the expense of another. Never laugh at a funeral. Never laugh at your own jokes. And never...

"No matter how many times I tell our mutual friend to never explain his jokes, Mr. McGill refuses to see that—in the approximate words of the famous writer, E.B. White—while humor can be dissected like a frog in a Biology lab, it dies in the process and the innards are discouraging to anyone other than... Of course, Possum is both a veterinary doctor and a taxidermist, so what can one expect?"

Max, more discouraged, again looked at his watch.

"Humor is no joke, Mr. Morgan, as dramatized by the old movie titled *The Name of the Rose* in which a Medieval Franciscan friar, with the help of a young novice such as yourself, rescued a long lost book penned by the Classical master, Aristotle—the *Second Book of Poetics*—extolling the virtues of funny. Church authorities during the infamous Inquisition believed laughter and jocularity were instruments of the Devil and..."

Feeling like he was back in school, Max began to squirm.

"As summed-up by the friar to his young novice, quote:

'Laughter kills fear, and without fear there would be no need for faith in God.'"

Under pressure of what Quinzel had called "performance anxiety", Max was ready to throw in a towel, but...

"Before I give up on you, Mr. Morgan, turn that frown upside down, suck it up and give me a full-blown belly laugh for which you are so physically well equipped to deliver."

"HA! HA! HA!"

"NO! NO! NO! Loud and emphatic, but a guffaw, not genuinely 'hearty' and not...What's that you're doing with your hand beneath your jacket?"

"Well, I'm a little nervous and..."

"One cannot induce laughter by attempting to physically tickle oneself. Interaction with a situation or series of events as imagined, or staged or humorously described by another is required to get a rise out of one's funny bone."

"That's what she said!"

Told that his case was as hopeless as that of Possum McGill, Max shuffled from the "stage", so to speak, like an unfunny comedian under a barrage of rotten tomatoes.

CHAPTER FOUR

♫My grandpa said go out and tell 'em a joke/ But be sure to give it plenty of hoke…♫

As his brother-in-law, Phil Phillips, gabbed with a pawn shop walk-in, Leo watched a familiar old video clip on a dusty VHS player that some poor sap had hocked likely decades ago. Though put out long before his time, the *Make 'Em Laugh* musical movie had made a fateful impression on him when he first saw it, and was still inspiring.

♫If you become a doctor, folks'll face you with dread/ If you become a dentist, they'll be glad when you're dead/ You'll get a bigger hand if you can stand on your head…♫

As a teenager he'd been big for his age and, not self-centered but self conscious. Deep inside, he had been, not insecure, but shy. Though liked, by hindsight Leo now realized he had not been well liked.

His tenth grade English teacher, for instance, had accused him of being a bully for de-pantsing Possum McGill during class, and sent him to the Principal's office for a stern talking-to. But what the hell, he'd thought it was a compliment to be compared to "Brom Bones", a schoolbook's hero who "got the girl" by playing tricks on a character called Ichabod Crane that finally drove the nerdy rival for the girl to flee from town in terror.

♫Make 'em roar, make 'em scream/ Take a fall, butt a wall, split a seam…♫

And for crying out loud, because Possum McGill was a runt—and thought of by some girls as "cute"—the pathetic little rodent got away with telling dirty knock-knock jokes that, when he himself cracked them, made girls act like they didn't like him. Even Lil Fox—though liking him a lot—had let McGill get into her pants and... Phew! But for making "withdrawals" instead of "deposits", he himself could've been institutionalized in marriage.

Instead, after getting out of the Army he had found his true love, in sales. Like someone famously said, for a salesman there was no rock bottom to the life. A salesman didn't put a bolt to a nut, didn't spout law or medicine. A salesman was a man out there in the blue, riding on a smile and a shoeshine. Door-to-door... on the phone...occasionally inside stores, he had sold everything from sets of pots-and-pans...to used cars...to life insurance...to hair-growth products...to women's shoes...you name it. Always on a straight-commission basis that allowed a go-getter like himself to bring in the green, but...

Sometimes prospective customers didn't smile back. Having doors slammed in his face...being hung-up on...seeing shoppers walk out after hearing his sales pitches... Well, despite a smile and a shoeshine, repeated rejection took its toll on a guy's self confidence. During a particularly prolonged dry spell... holed up in a run-down out-of-the-way motel in the middle of a gloomy night... watching an old movie on tv...

♫Give 'em quips, give 'em fun/ And they'll say you're A-One...♫

Bingo.

♫Make 'em laugh, make 'em laugh, make 'em laugh...♫

At a secondhand bookstore, in exchange for his collection of how-to sales manuals—*Wait, There's More* by the legendary Ron Popell... *Make an Offer They Can't Refuse* by the also legendary Gil Gunderson... and numerous others—he'd snagged a single dog-eared paperback copy of *Stolen Jokes* by a guy named Milton Berle. And as fate would have it, an old VHS tape...

♫Make 'em laugh, make 'em laugh, make 'em laugh...♫

Humor was the ticket to getting a foot in the door... to keeping a prospect on the line...to detaining female shoe shoppers long enough to close a sale. Sure, some customers, a lot of them actually, had laughed in his face. But not anymore.

Not that even super-salesmen didn't also have ups-and-downs. During a current lull in demand for damned near everything, he had agreed—at the insistence of his sister, Barbara Jo—to work as an armed security guard at his brother-in-law's pawn shop until...

"Hey, Leo, come over here and meet Harold Finegan," Phil hollered from across the shop. And after he'd joined them at the cash register, "You two may be just what the other is looking for," his brother-in-law added.

"Leo Wolfe," said Leo, applying a vise-like handshake as recommended by Gil Gunderson. "But please, Harold, just call me loud-and-clear when the bartender announces 'last call', ha, ha, ha," he continued, as recommended by Gunderson for breaking ice. "Which reminds me, ever hear the one about the drunk Irishman who walked into a bar...a chair... and a wall? Ha, ha, ha..."

"Mr. Finegan owns the Acme Industrial Supply Company," said Phil, "and is in need of a sales rep to..."

"Say no more. Leo Wolfe is a bang-beat, big-haul, rip-roarin', every-time-a- bullseye salesman, and I happen to be currently..."

"The job mainly involves just calling on established machine shop customers in the eastern part of the state and into Arkansas," said Finegan. "Just stocking shelves with our lines of cutting tools, nuts, bolts, screws, and the occasional anvil. Just taking orders and..."

"And always leaving 'em laughing. Ol' Leo knows the territory like Adam 'knew' Eve in the Bible, ha, ha, ha. And I put my mouth where I bring in the green, by working on win-win straight commission."

"Well, like I say..."

"Speaking of nuts and cutting tools, by the way, ever hear the one about the guy who went to a doctor for a circumcision, looked down after surgery and saw..."

"Like I say, the job involves mainly just calling on established customers and re-filling orders. So it's a salaried position that…"

"Never take a sale for granted," Leo advised, as his brother-in-law rolled his eyes for some reason. "To hold on to regular customers, a salesman has to be not just liked, but well liked. Which means a salesman has to have a gift for funny gab. Ever hear the one about the traveling salesman and the farmer's two daughters?"

Ignoring a throat-cutting gesture made by his clueless brother-in-law. Leo set up a sure-fire joke, then closed:

"So the farmer wrote a letter to the traveling salesman that said: 'Was it you who did the pushin' with my youngest daughter on the cushion, left your footprints on the wall upside down? Since you left my darling Nelly, she's had swelling of her belly, so I think that you should come around.' Ha, ha, ha…"

"Leo, Mr. Finegan is a…"

"The salesman wrote back, and said: 'Yeah, and it was also me who did the pushin' with your other daughter on the cushion, and left more footprints on the wall upside down. But since I met your darling Venus I've had red spots on my penis, so I'd say we're Even-Steven all around.' Ha, ha, ha…"

"I myself live on a farm, Mr. Wolfe," said his prospective new employer, but without so much as the crack of a smile on his face. "And I happen to have two daughters."

Though he had succeeded in finding a subject of common interest, which was the second rule of salesmanship…

"I'll have to think it over," the humorless nuts-and-bolts guy said, before turning away and marching out of the pawn shop.

"Damnit, Leo, how many times do I have to tell you that you talk too much, glad-hand too much, and don't close sales that are there to be made," said his brother-in-law, whose sales know-how consisted of haggling with poor saps wanting to redeem already cherished stuff such as old VHS players and tapes they'd pawned during dry spells. "Like they say, Bro, everybody may like a kidder, but nobody lends him money."

Returned to his post near the shop entrance, Leo's self confidence, even a few drops of self esteem, drained into his shoes. He was well liked, he reminded himself, but...He had been out of a sales job for almost a year and...For crying out loud, though he'd dropped hints that today was his birthday, and had expected to be 'surprised' with at least a cupcake at this morning's gathering of Furries...

Buzz. Buzz. Buzz...

Leo looked at his phone, and...Aha. Finally, a come-on from Lil McGill *nee* Fox, the bygone Queen of the Senior Prom who—before he got good at cracking jokes—had picked Possum McGill instead of him. Now, heh, heh, heh, ol' Leo would have the last laugh.

CHAPTER FIVE

Max parked his mom's brown Buick boiler around the corner from the McGill residence as instructed, got out of the ride, and put on the headpiece of his rented costume.

The Furries' birthday party for Leo Wolfe had been set up by Possum as a surprise. No presents, just "bring yourself," he'd been told. So Yours Truly's contribution to the festive affair would be limited to laughing at jokes, some of which — thanks to a couple of hours of online research — he himself would tell. To warm up...

"Knock, knock," he nervously muttered to himself as he ankled toward the darkened party scene.

"Who's there?" he muttered.

"Hoppy."

"Hoppy who?"

"Hop-pee birthday potty."

"He, heh, heh..."

Knock, knock.

The door opened, and inside a dimly candlelit living room...

"Is that you, Max?" said someone. "What's with the bear outfit? Didn't you get the memo?"

Ha, ha, ha, ha, ha...

Uh oh. Seeing that McGill was not decked out as a possum... that Bill Roberts was not sporting even bunny ears... that everyone was wearing ordinary clothes...that Yours Truly was the butt of a joke...Max took off the furry bear head.

"Yep, it's Br'er Bear alright," Wiley "Coyote" Johnson confirmed.

"Heck, Max, you could get shot walking around after dark in that costume," said Possum.

"Yeah, knock knock," said Scratchy Katz, "and when the other guy says, 'I've been shot...'"

"'I've been shot?' the door knocker says." said Possum. "'You think this is a joke?'"

Ha, ha, ha, ha, ha...

"Yo mama so slow, it took her nine months to deliver a joke!"

Ha, ha, ha, ha, ha...

"Put your head back on, Br'er Bear. It'll scare the preserves out of Wolfie."

Ha, ha, ha, ha, ha...

Max noticed a large cake displayed on a dining-nook table... ankled over to see if it was real or, by the look of it, a cardboard fake...and detected the faint whine of something—or someone—trapped inside the party decor. A smaller real cake with a candle stuck on top...

"Shhh!" Rabbit Roberts shushed from his lookout post beside a window. "Wolfie's car just parked at the curb."

"Snuff the candles and open the front door a crack," Possum ordered.

Max put on his furry costume's headpiece, held his breath and...

"Knock, knock, anybody home?"

The living room lights came on.

Surprise!

Bang!

"What the hell!" said Leo Wolfe, standing there with a smoking gun in hand.

Max patted-down himself, detected no wounds, but...

"I've been shot!" Possum wailed.

Ha, ha, ha, ha, ha...

"How are we going to bury the body?" said someone.

Ha, ha, ha...

"Alpaca shovel," said someone else.

Ha, ha, ha...

"You think this is a joke?" said Possum. "Look at the blood on my pants."

"It was an accident!" Wolfe yelped, dropping the handgun onto the floor. "Who's the dumbass in the bear suit who...who startled me?"

"Possum said it was to be a surprise costume party," said Max, after again taking off the head of his costume. "And...And I was never good at catching onto jokes."

"Yeah, sure, play dumber than you are and try to put the blame on Possum," said Wolfe, glaring at him. "It's your fault, Morgan."

"Somebody call the cops!"

"Somebody call a doctor!"

"No!" Possum barked. "No cops, and no docs. It's just a flesh wound, and Lil will be home soon to take care of things. I don't want anyone else taking my pants off."

"Good thinking, old friend," Wolfe agreed, before visually surveying the room and adding: "To avoid this...this incident becoming a federal case against Morgan, well, it could have been that Possum was, uh, cleaning the gun and it went off. Right? That's our story, and we stick to it."

"Yeah, let's all get out of here and let Possum's Missus examine his private parts."

"We're not doctors."

"And we're not queers."

At the wheel of the brown boiler, racing homeward with chilly air blowing through a side window, memory of a high school "snipe hunt" came to Max's mind. Hopefully, he would again turn out to be only the butt of a joke that tomorrow would be the subject of Furries cachinnation.

THURSDAY

November 20, 2025

CHAPTER SIX

Following a sleepless night of worry, Max ankled into the local police station. His mom—with whom he had lived since birth—had ordered him to report last night's, uh, incident involving Possum McGill, Leo Wolfe, and, dang it, Yours Truly. Mom was almost always right, but...

"Any overnight 911 calls about gunshot incidents?" he asked the cop on counter duty, a *faux* flatfoot named Williams.

"Why do you ask?" said the local Barney Fife. "Hear something go 'bang' in the dark?"

"Just wondering if. . . Yours Truly is a private dick, ya know. Keeping an eye, ear, and nose in the air goes with the territory."

"Look, listen, scratch-'n'-sniff outside, Morgan. I've got paperwork to do."

Semi-relieved that no news was good news, Max faded the cop coop and ankled along Main Street toward the Mister Quickie copy shop, where a workstation cubicle served as his office. He didn't want to come across to fellow Furries as a guy who couldn't take a joke and laugh at his own foible, but...

Inside the cubicle, the teenaged kid—a wannabe P.I. who served as his case report jotter in the mode of a Dr. Watson, an Agatha Christie, a Mickey Spillane-- had plopped his also over-sized derriere in the client chair. After parking his own double-wide butt at his desk...

"What's up, Mr. Max?" said the kid. "You don't have a best friend, but if you did, you look like you've just lost him."

Possum McGill was not really a "best" friend and, hopefully, not "lost". But after unloading on the young jotter about the incident at last night's surprise birthday party for Leo Wolfe...

"Hmmm," the kid hmmmed. "If it was you in costume that Mr. Wolfe mistook for a bear, why would he have shot Mr. McGill?"

"Listen-and-learn, kid. Wolfe is only a security guard at his brother-in-law's pawn shop. When confronted by...a bear, civilians don't shoot straight."

"Or the lead that hit Possum could have been a ricochet.

"Or the incident could have been staged as a kind of initiation into the Furries to see if Yours Truly has a funny bone."

"Yeah, but even if it was a joke, or maybe an accident, my advice, Mr.Max, is that you play along and dope out what went down. In Mr. Percy Wilson's *Case of Just for Laughs* a clown faked a slip on a banana peel and hit the savvy detective in the face with a poisoned pie."

Hmmm.

After the kid hustled off to school, Max got off his backside... exited Quickie's...and ankled along Main Street toward the Wide-O-Wake Cafe. At the entrance to the Furries hang-out, he took a deep breath. Inside the joint...

Ha, ha, ha, ha, ha, ha, ha...

At sight and sound of the corner table no change to regulars, jolly as ever, he heaved a sigh of relief. but...

Ha, ha, ha, ha, ha, ha, ha...

At sight of two empty chairs at the table, and no sign of Possum McGill...

Ha, ha, ha, ha, ha, ha, ha...

...he heaved a sigh of unrelief.

"Join the party, Br'er Bear," Leo Wolfe bellowed. "All is forgiven. Ha, ha, ha...I was just telling the boys about the blonde whose hubby seemed to have died of a heart attack during sex, ha, ha, ha...The 911 operator told her the first thing to do was make sure her hubby was dead and...Bang! 'Okay, now what?' said the blonde."

Ha, ha, ha, ha, ha, ha, ha...

"Speaking of 'bangs in the night', any word about Possum?"

"Shhh," Wolfe shushed. "It takes a high-speed vehicle on a

highway to kill a possum, which is why redneck chefs call blue-plate specials 'roasted roadkill'."

Ha, ha, ha, ha, ha, ha, ha...

"Yeah, roasted possum smells like possum, but tastes like squirrel," said Coyote Johnson.

But Yours Truly was the only one who laughed.

"For formal initiation into the Furries, tell us a funny one, Bear," said Rabbit Roberts.

Back to semi-relieved, but nervous, Max wracked his brain and finally...

"There was another hubby, caught *en fragrante* with another dame by another blonde wife, and...and...I can't remember exactly what happened, but believe me, fellas, it was funny. Ha, ha, ha..."

No one else even faked a laugh, not even a chortle, not even a....

"You must be thinking of the one about the brunette, friend of a blonde, who invited the blonde's hubby to come by her house," said Rabbit. "When he got there, she gave him the come-on, told him to go into a dark room and..."

"Surprise!" Leo roared. "Lights came on and the poor sap—standing there in his birthday suit—realized he was the guest of honor at a party!"

Ha, ha, ha, ha, ha, ha, ha...

Birthday suit? Max didn't see the humor, but played along.

"But you can't fool ol' Leo," ol' Leo continued. "When Lil invited me to drop by, I smelled something fishy and..."

"Yeah, smells like fish, tastes like chicken," Coyote Johnson howled. "Ha, ha, ha..."

"She said..."

"What have you sons-of-bitches done with Possum?!" said Lil McGill, Possum's Missus, suddenly standing at the table with hands on her hips and an angry look on her kisser.

"The living room is an f'ing mess!"

Uh oh. Max doped out that Possum McGill must have crawled through and from the house, bleeding, and had probably ended toes-up on a highway.

CHAPTER SEVEN

Leo jumped to his feet, raised his arms and…and…and faced with Lil's angry accusative glare, couldn't bring to mind a joke to lighten the mood. Instead…

"Don't look at me, Lil," he said. "The living room was tidy as an Army barracks when I left last night."

"Tidy?! When I got home the floor was littered with a dead beaver and…"

Dead beaver?

"…blood…cardboard scraps…cake crumbs…and a gun."

"Possum must have shot the beaver later," said Scratchy Katz. "Probably he planned…I mean, plans to stuff it."

"Then 'mount' it," Rabbit cracked. "Ha, ha, ha…"

"Possum is nowhere to be found, his phone is dead, and…"

Dead!

"…my so-called husband doesn't own a gun, and neither do I."

Uh oh.

"The beaver likely jumped out of the cardboard cake, like the bastard wanted <u>me</u> to do. And someone…"

"Lucky that you backed out, Lil," said Leo. "Heh, heh, let's look on the bright side. Let's have a laugh at Possum's pathetic attempted joke. Heh, heh…"

"Yeah, lucky it wasn't you who didn't want us to get into <u>your</u> pants, Lil," said Rabbit. "Ha, ha, ha…"

"We're not doctors, but…"

"We're queers. Ha, ha, ha…"

"Yeah, you got lucky, Sister," the fat Notary Public needlessly added. "It could have been you who crawled…"

"Uh huh, the little wimp probably 'crawled' back to mommy in Tulsa," Lil snorted. "The wicked witch never approved of me, and Possum never wanted to leave her pouch."

With his footing back to steady, Leo again tried to think of an appropriate joke. Getting a laugh out of a woman meant a guy was halfway there, but… His brain, as though having a mind of its own:

Murder of a friend by a friend is called homiecide.
Jokes are funny 'til someone gets hurt, then hilarious.
Otherwise, how did you enjoy the theater, Mrs. Lincoln?
Drop the gun, not your pants, said the female cop.
But when a guy gets all the way there, a woman's laugh…

Hmmm. Was he himself being made the butt of a joke?

Nah, not ol' Leo. Under the right circumstances, Lil would jump at an opportunity to pop out of a fake cake for him. And not just for laughs. But why would Possum…?

Hmmm.

The little rodent—Possum, not the beaver—would have expected him to be startled and… Yeah, McGill must have known Lil was still hot for him, the King of the Prom and now funnier than ever. Lil must have backed out of the "surprise" party set-up…

"If my husband is not back home by end of the day, I'm going to the cops," the real "Beaver" was now saying. "So you sons-of-bitches had better get your story straight," she declared, before storming out of the cafe.

"It's all your fault, Morgan," said Leo. "Right, boys? You saw Morgan stupidly jump at me."

"Yeah, Max, you made Leo think you were a bear," Rabbit agreed, getting up from the table.

"But…But…But…" the fatso stammered.

"Don't call me 'butt'," Leo reflexively replied, but…but… but…

One-by-one, the others claimed they had to get back to work and, like firemen called to a five-alarm blaze…Suddenly,

Leo found himself all alone, with nowhere to go, nobody to see, nothing to…Like someone said, the only thing a man had in this world was something to sell, but for almost a year now…

He didn't really have a job, not even as a security guard for his brother-in-law. Other than the *Make 'Em Laugh* VHS tape, there was nothing in the pawn shop worth stealing. The only time he'd handled redemption of hocked collateral —a treasured family Bible—the guy had changed his mind. But…Damnit, 'ol Leo was a never-say-die salesman. Like the dyslexic guy, when life served him melons…

♪*Be a clown, be a clown, all the world loves a clown/ Show 'em tricks, tell 'em jokes…*♪

Hell, they made operas and movies about salesmen and, okay, clowns, who were down on their luck. Envious others…

♪*A butcher or a baker, ladies never embrace/ But they'll all come to call if you can fall on your face…*♪

He was not a clown, not a pathetic bozo like that Italian singer who got all weepy when life served up a melon. Ol' Leo was funny, well liked by everyone he met. But…

♪*Give em quips, give 'em fun, and they'll say you're A-One…*♪

Somewhat like the poor sap in another famous old movie, Leo had a depressing feeling that he was not needed anymore, that a smile and a shoeshine and a bag of gags were no longer…

He blamed what they called "globalization" for the death of salesmanship. Hell, nowadays a person in Henryetta, Oklahoma could pick up a phone to place an order and find himself talking to someone in India who barely spoke understandable English, and had no gift for gab. How could anyone like, much less well like a foreigner? And on the home front, Amazon made it easy for customers to buy things without opening the doors of their houses except for deliveries of everything and anything: sets of pots-and-pans…women's shoes…hair growth products…life insurance policies…even cars!

Leo sighed.

As a salesman, on the road for most of thirty years, what did he have to show for all those days knocking on doors, all those lonely nights in cheap motels? A life insurance policy he had sold to himself to meet a quota, that was all. He was worth more dead than alive.

♫*Make 'em laugh, make 'em laugh/ Everyone wants to laugh…* ♫

He blamed so-called political correctness for the decline and near-death of laughter. Hell, even professional comedians—Jerry Seinfeld, for instance, and others—now avoided even college-campus gigs. Most of what people used to laugh at was mostly so-called "ethnic humor", people laughing at themselves and, okay, laughing at the, uh, peculiarities of others. Some said jokes told by Jewish people about themselves were a way of coping with melons.

"I'm tired and thirsty,' said the Italian. 'I must have wine.' And the Jewish guy says, 'I'm tired and thirsty. I must have diabetes.'"

"I have good news,' said the rabbi to a group fearfully huddled inside a synagogue during a pogrom. 'The murdered girl was Jewish!'

""You said Goldman doesn't live here,' said the cop. "'You call this living?' Goldman answered.

"I don't deserve this award,' said Groucho Marx, 'but I have arthritis and don't deserve that either.'"

Realizing that he had been talking out loud to himself, not a good sign… "Hey, Charlie," Leo hollered at the cafe counter man, "c'mon over here and take a load off. Life is short, like a good joke. Which reminds me, ever hear the one about the traveling salesman who comes home a day early, finds his wife wearing a negligee, and his best friend inside a closet wearing a…?"

"Too busy, Leo. And as a matter of fact, yeah, you told that one yesterday, and the day before."

Leo blamed the internet for the current dearth of jocularity. Hell, nowadays a guy could come up with a joke or hear one on tv, put it out there in space, and all of a sudden everyone in the world had read or heard it, more than once or twice. So-called AI—hell, intelligence, artificial or otherwise—was like death to a sense of humor. And almost all jokes found on the internet were either too mean-spirited or too dirty to tell in a group and risk getting sued or...

He had never liked Dan McGill, and Lil knew it. Though hot for ol' Leo, she had married the hopeless loser out of spite for... Okay, back in high school he'd not realized that girls believed promises made in the heat of moments. Lil was still mad, and McGill—to spite him for being the love of her life—was probably now pouting, "playing possum" literally. But...

Leo stood up from the cafe table like a...like a clown hit in the face with a pie. If McGill didn't show up alive and none the worse for wear...If Lil went to the police...If cops started asking questions...Off he went, to make the most important sales pitch of his life.

CHAPTER EIGHT

Back at his Mister Quickie workstation, Max Googled "Frances 'Bunny' MacDougal"…got a telephone number…and put in a call. Possum McGill's mother—a former member of his own mom's Canasta club—had remarried, moved to Tulsa, and…

"Make it short-and-sweet," said a raspy woman's voice. "Who's dead?"

Without mention of the, uh, incident at the surprise birthday party for Leo Wolfe that might have distressed the elderly broad, "Just a beaver, so far," said Max, "but I thought you should know."

"You interrupted my tv show to report a dead beaver?"

"Well, I know you must worry about Possum, and…Oh yeah, he didn't make it home last night, so some of us were just wondering…"

"Home! You call living with that sly foxy woman a home? I warned Daniel about that little minx and sure enough, she tricked him into marriage to spite me. My son is a doctor, you know. He could have had any wife I approved of. He could have provided me with grandchildren more respectable than that one-and-only offspring who joined a circus and became a clown, for christsake."

"So you've not seen or heard from Daniel?"

"Not since he called yesterday afternoon. But I'm not worried if that's what you're wondering. I'm hopeful my son has finally come to his senses, and run off with that Miss Filmore he talks so fondly about. Daniel is still not too old to provide…"

Miss Filmore?

"As for that other one, better she was never an unwanted in-law of mine. Better she had remained an outlaw."

Outlaw?

Before he could grill her, Old Lady MacDougal *nee* Old Lady McGill said she was in the middle of a *Sex in the City* re-run and abruptly ended the call.

Hmmm.

With the plot of Possum McGill's disappearance thickened, Max got up from his desk...exited Quickie's...and hotfooted along Main Street.

In a matter of minutes, he arrived   at a whitewashed cinderblock building on the east side of downtown, identified by a high pole-mounted sign as :

ANIMAL HOSPITAL & TAXIDERMY LAB

And on a separate billboard:

SAVE UR PETS

Dead or Alive

Inside a small reception area, he detected yelps coming from a back room... an array of stuffed animals on shelves and a counter...and unpleasant odor. But no hide nor hair of Possum McGill, alive or dead.

"Doctor is not in today," said a mousy-looking dame, coming from the back room in a starchy white outfit that looked to be bloodstained. In reply to his grilling, "He's probably just not feeling up to snuff due to the death of Miss Fiimore."

Miss Filmore was dead?

"Mrs. McGill came by earlier with the carcass."

Carcass?

"So sad. Doctor loved that beaver."

Miss Filmore was a beaver?

"Beavers are not underline{un}affectionate. They like being petted. But they can't be trained, won't come when you want them to, won't tolerate a leash. And Miss Filmore had a voracious appetite for more wood than Doctor could provide."

For some reason, *Case of the Naked Gun* came to mind, but...

"Doctor must have decided the only way to keep her was to stuff her."

"You telling me the 'doc' shot Miss... the beaver, in cold blood?"

"Oh no, Doctor hates guns. Yesterday was a year to the day that he rescued Miss Filmore. To mark the occasion, he must have put the poison in a what you might call a surprise birthday cake. Her mouth was almost full of unenjoyed pink crumbs, poor dear."

Max ankled out onto the Main Street sidewalk, wondering: Lil McGill was the proprietor of the C-Cups Cakes & Coffee bakery cafe at the west end of Main Street. No doubt she had baked the cupcake with a candle in it that had sat on the table next to the large cardboard fake cake likely containing Miss Filmore.

Hmmm.

McGill had always been an odd duck, not the kind of guy likely to have much luck with dames, but...Was the Missus jealous of her husband's "fond relationship" with the beaver?

Max ducked into Town Hall, where Bill Roberts kept track of official documents. Due to Yours Truly' Notary Public stamping services, "Rabbit" was the Furry he knew best, and a longtime friend of Possum McGill. At a counter...

"Possum didn't show up at his mom's house in Tulsa last night," he reported. "And didn't shown up for work this morning."

"Uh oh," said Roberts.

"And get this: McGill seems to have been, uh, affectionately captivated with that beaver and his Missus..."

"Well yeah, they've been married for quite a while now, but even so..."

"Possum married Miss Filmore?!"

"Miss Filmore? Heck no, Possum married Lil Fox right after high school. I think it was Leo who started calling her 'Beaver', probably because of her buck teeth, and...Heck, Lil was Queen of the Senior Prom, Leo was King, and Possum was... just Possum. No one understood why she picked him instead of Leo."

Hmmm.

Max's brain—that he sometimes thought of as a hamster

inside his head—began to spin a wheel, and…As Charlie Chan famously observed in *Case of Geometry for Dummies,* "Love triangles often become wrecktangles."

Hmmm.

Another documentary from back in the murky *Noir* came to mind: In *Case of Another Man's Poison* a married dame got into an affectionate relationship with another man. When a joker showed up, claiming to be her strayed husband, she poured poison from a flask into his drink. But then a nosy neighbor—who happened to be an animal doctor—reported that her real husband had in fact returned. She fainted. And when the vet revived her—by pouring the remaining flask contents down her gullet—the deadly dame ended up laughing hysterically.

Hmmm.

Max had a hunch Possum McGill might have become confused after being gunshot, might have nibbled on the poisoned cupcake and, well, according to the expert, Frances Quinzel, some people literally died in fits of cachinnation.

CHAPTER NINE

♫*If I could turn back time, if I could find a way/ Maybe, maybe, maybe...*"

In the so-called living room under the roof she'd shared with Possum McGill since what seemed the beginning of time, Lil again nipped "courage" from a flask while again looking back on how she had come to think of herself as the pathetic Lorraine Baines *nee* McFly in the *Back to the Future* movies.

As a silly teenaged girl with her nose out of joint she had talked herself into believing that—as dramatized in *BTTF I*—Possum had rescued her from Leo Wolfe's abusive treatment... that the high school class nerd would go on to become a successful heart surgeon...that her mother was right in counseling that she would learn to love him...and that she would forget about Leo. But...

♫*I don't know why I did the things I did/I don't know why I said the things I said...* ♫

Years later, she'd tried to believe that Leo was a bully...that if he killed Possum back then and she had become Mrs. Wolfe after all—as dramatized in *BTTF II*—he would have become a wealthy, but crooked businessman...unfaithful...truly abusive... and that she would have been even more miserable. But the fantasizing hadn't worked. Her true feelings hadn't changed. Now Leo was a successful salesman, passing through town and...

She'd not seen him except in passing. Except for briefly on the phone yesterday to suit Possum, they hadn't talked. But she'd keenly felt the "Wild Thing's" presence—yes, "Wild Thing" was Leo's private nickname—mainly by way of Possum's accounts of regular gatherings of "Furries", including obviously mangled repetition of Leo's jokes in which he—her pathetic husband—was the clueless butt. She had lacked the "courage" to engage, though yearning to re-connect and...

♪*If I could turn back time, if I could find a way/ Maybe, maybe, maybe you'd stay...* ♫

Ding. Dong.

Lil went to the door...opened it and...as though miraculously returned from out of the past...there stood Leo, with a bouquet of flowers in hand. Expecting delivery of a joke...

"Lil, we need to talk," he said, brushing past her into the house, then turning to thrust the bouquet at her. "I came by to say I'm sorry for..."

"After all these years? Is that an apology?"

"Well, yeah, 'I'm sorry' and 'I apologize' mean the same thing, except at a funeral. Ha, ha, ha..."

"Not funny, Leo. The beaver is dead. Possum would have taken it hard and..."

"That's an old one, Lil: the dishes might pile up, but the sex will be the same and...Sorry, bad timing. Otherwise, how did you enjoy the play, Mrs...?"

"Why do you make a joke about...about everything?" she asked, though knowing the reason no doubt better than he did. Beneath the surface, Leo had always been insecure. Cracking jokes had always been his way of hiding true feelings. Attempts at making people laugh had been his pathetic way of trying to be liked.

"It was dark in here," he said, pacing. "The lights came on and...and...and that fat Notary Public, Max Morgan—wearing a bear suit, for crying out loud—startled me. Like the bear who walked into a bar, ordered three shots and the bartender...What happened to Possum was Morgan's fault, damnit!"

"What <u>did</u> 'happen' to Possum?"

"It was an accident, Lil. Like the time Possum fell out of that tree while window-peeping, and asked to be taken to the ICU. Ha, ha...Not that Possum needed to go to a hospital this time. In fact, he wouldn't let us call a doctor...or the police. That might have been his, uh, final wish, Lil. We owe it to Possum to not get cops involved."

Lil was not surprised, nor upset by Leo's confession. To the contrary, given the opportunity to make her uncaring high school boyfriend pay for leaving her in a lurch…

"All the magazine articles say there are no accidents," she said. "And no doubt it's not just me, but also others wondering why you came back to town and continued to hang around."

"My brother-in-law needed…Well, to tell the truth…"

"To torment me is the obvious answer, and to get back at Possum for me having him as a mate instead of you."

Expecting an attempted humorous comeback, Lil was surprised — and viciously delighted — to see Leo Wolfe collapse onto a love seat, bury his face in his hands, and mumble that he was "down on his luck"…that it had been a year since he'd "closed a sale"…and that "no one liked him anymore".

"I admit, there have been times when I wanted to kill Possum," he continued after looking up to her. "I just couldn't believe that you liked him better than me. And when the lights came on, when I saw Possum sitting here on this love seat, where the two of you must have…I've been wishing I could turn back the clock and…The gun went off. I didn't intend to…"

Lil, suddenly enflamed, tossed the bouquet aside…ripped off her clothes and…in a frenzied release of pent up desire… fell into the almost open arms of the long-lost love of her life. Like a pair of wild animals…What joy!…What bliss!…What ecstasy!…What…

Ding. Dong.

Oh no, had Possum survived?…Had he lost his key?…Was her husband at the door, armed with one of his sharp taxidermy tools?

"Quick!" she barked at Leo as she gathered herself. "Hide in the closet!"

"Is this a joke?" he said, doing as instructed. "Is his the one about…?

Bang!

After slamming the closet door shut, Lil—dressed but flustered—tidied her clothes and hair…went to the front door… took a deep breath and…

"Sorry to barge in," said the fat man who claimed to be a private detective. "I'm looking into the suspicious disappearance of your Mister. Have a few questions about how poison got into one of your C-Cup cupcakes."

CHAPTER TEN

"Is this some kind of joke?"

Max brushed off the the attempted dodge by Possum McGill's obviously nervous Missus...returned to the living room table where "Miss Filmore" must have been confined inside the fake cardboard cake...recalled spotting a cupcake with a candle on top that the escaped beaver must have chowed down on...and followed a trail of crumbs, so to speak.

"The joke's on you, Sweetheart," he said, back in the cunning C-Cup cooker's face. "Yours Truly has studied almost all the pulp case reports of private dick investigations dating back to the *Noir* and beyond. Nine out of ten times poison — nonviolent, bloodless, and sneaky — is a dame's murrrderrr method."

"'Murrrderrr'?"

"Yeah, your missing husband is likely lying toes-up in the woods by now, done in by the poisoned pastry you cooked up for him."

"Don't be ridiculous. That beaver may have nibbled on 'the cupcake, and may have ingested poison from...from some source, but..."

"Yeah, two rodents with one stone, so to speak. Possum was 'fond' of Miss Filmore."

"You call yourself a private 'dick'?" the feisty *femme fatale* snorted, with *mea culpa* written on her kisser in plain English. "Yes, I baked the cupcake, but not for my husband. Leo Wolfe was the birthday boy. We're old friends and I thought..."

Max detected what sounded like a slightly muffled guffaw. Then...

"This is <u>not</u> that old joke!"

The unmuffled shout came from…Leo Wolfe, half-dressed, looked to have been searching in a closet for something to put on.

"I'm not an exterminator, and don't claim that moths ate my shorts!"

Hmmm.

"For crying out loud, Lil, why? A birthday cupcake for 'ol Leo, I get that. But poison! I made those promises in the heat of moments almost thirty years ago. I came back to you and…"

"He came back to town, still enflamed with…with jealousy that's been festering like…like poison ever since I married Possum instead of him," said Lil McGill, pointing a finger at Wolfe. "Just minutes ago he said he's been wanting to kill my husband, and confessed…"

"I said I was sorry, and we were not talking about Possum at his funeral!"

"Don't try the old religious dodge on Yours Truly," said Max. "That's a closet, not one of those church booths where confessions made in heat don't cut ice in court."

"Talk about heat of moments! Minutes ago she jumped me on that love seat," Wolfe claimed, pointing a finger at Possum McGill's likely widow. "Everybody knows she's been unhappily married for years, and still has the hots for ol' Leo."

"How dare you try to blame me, you bastard! You shot Possum and…"

"I was startled by…You were here, Morgan. You saw that… that the gun went off. It was an accident, and not my fault."

"Leo would not have been 'startled'. I called him earlier at my husband's request, to tease…but changed my mind and spoiled Possum's planned surprise by warning the bastard that 'Miss Filmore'…"

"Dang it, I wish you hadn't done that Lil," said…not Wolfe, but McGill, coming through a doorway into the living room with, uh oh, a gun in hand. "I wanted to give Leo a comeuppance for all the times he made me the butt of his jokes."

"Possum!" Wolfe hollered with upraised arms. "Whatcha been up to, Bro? A tree, hanging from a limb, window-peeking on naked bathing beauties like you used to? Ha, ha, ha…"

"You peeped too, Leo Wolfe, I knew you were out there," said Lil McGill, before rushing toward her returned husband with open arms. "Don't listen to a word he says, Honey."

McGill ignored the wife, glared at Wolfe, and said: "Actually, I have been out in the woods, hanging out and thinking about things."

Despite his Missus saying that things were "not what they seemed", and Wolfe adding "that's what makes things funny", the lucky survivor went on to tell that while "hanging out" in the woods overnight he'd realized:

One, that he'd been nowhere near what would have been the line of fire of Leo's shot at a "bear".

Hmmm.

Two, that he had never before known Leo to walk around armed, and recalled the pawn shop security guard complaining that his brother-in-law would not let him carry the weapon off pawn shop premises.

Hmmm.

Three, that he himself had always liked being with animals better than in the company of people…that he had married Lil only because she wanted him to, and cried about it…and that he had always wondered why Leon, the boy he raised as a son, had curly red hair and ran off to be a clown in a circus.

Uh oh, Leo Wolfe had curly red hair.

"Is this one of those old 'my-daddy-was-a-mailman' jokes, Possum?" said Wolfe. "Ha, ha, ha…"

"Yeah, an almost thirty-year-old joke," said McGill.

Hmmm.

Though Yours Truly had served a twenty-five-year stint in the U.S. Postal Service, half that time delivering mail, he didn't recall…

"But your gunshot only grazed my groin…I was fixing to put Miss Filmore to sleep and mount her anyway…and Leon will always be my boy. So…"

"In that case, as the traveling salesman said to the farmer…"

"It really is just a joke when you think about it," Possum surprisingly concluded, dropping the gun. "Ha, ha, ha…"

"OMG! You do have a funny bone after all," said Lil, hugging her husband. "Ha, ha, ha…"

"That's actually what she said," Max blurted.

Ha, ha, ha, ha, ha, ha, ha…

That was the punchline of the joke he'd botched yesterday morning at the cafe, and now…

Ha, ha, ha, ha, ha, ha, ha…

Max felt his larynx begin to close…his air intake becoming irregular…his mouth opening and closing in a struggle for oxygen…and to his surprise…

Ha, ha, ha, ha, ha, ha, ha…

…he realized tears were running down his cheeks as he joined in the infectious cachinnation.

Ha, ha, ha, ha, ha, ha, ha…

What joy…What bliss…What a relief!

Ha, ha, ha, ha, ha, ha, ha…

THE
END

WILLIAM LEROY

DECEMBER

DOG IN A BOX

All rights reserved. Published by Mossik Press.

mossikpress@mail.com

Library of Congress Cataloguing-in-Publication Data

LeRoy, William [12.5.2025]

Cachinnation / Doc In A Box
by William LeRoy

p. cm
ISBN 979-8-9992429-3-8

1. Humor—Fiction.
2. Oklahoma, United States—Fiction.
3. Mystery—Fiction.
4. Noir—Fiction.
I. Title

10 9 8 7 6 5 4 3 2 1

Manufactured in the United States of America
First Edition

DOC IN A BOX

DECEMBER

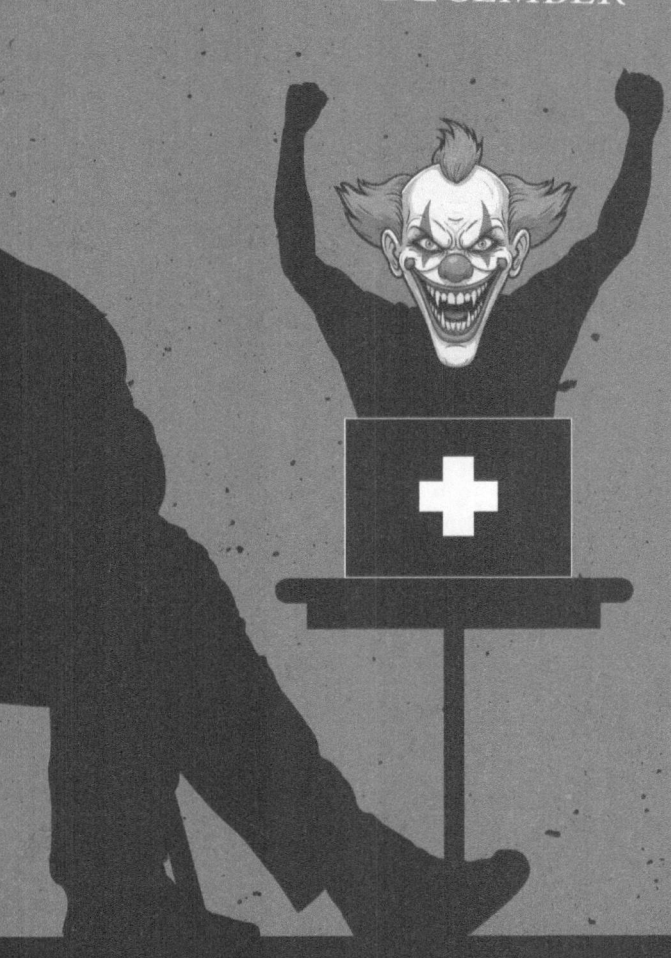

WILLIAM LEROY

TUESDAY

December 16, 2025

CHAPTER ONE

At his desk inside the Mister Quickie copy shop cubicle that served as his office, Max peered into a crystal ball, so to speak. According to an online ad, the website now glowing on the screen of his laptop computer—*blueprintincome.com*—would tell his future. So...

With prospects of upcoming fame-and-fortune in mind, he took a deep breath... and began to fill-in boxes:

PERSONAL INFORMATION
Gender: Male [X]
Race White [X]

AGE & PHYSIQUE
Age: [52]
Height: [5] feet [9] inches
Weight: [ ] pounds

Hmmm.

Max leaned back in his chair to noodle, not because he was negatively self conscious about his physique. He had been naturally born pear-shaped and overweight. As an adult, he had proudly modeled himself after Brad Runyon, a famous private detective from back in the *Noir* known as "The Fat Man". But ...

During annual physical check-ups, the local sawbones, Doc Sanders, had repeatedly lectured him about the effect of lard on...on his future, or lack of one. The doc had effectively warned that, without a change of "lifestyle", he would soon be physically "filling in a box", so to speak, for burial six-feet under.

On the other hand, his also chubby mom was now seventy-five and still going strong, so…

Weight:[243] pounds

LIFE EVENTS
Education:[X] High School Graduate
Maital Status:[X] Single
Employment: [   ] Currently Working [   ] Retired
Annual Income: [   ] - 40K []+40K

Hmmm.

He was both retired—from the U.S. Postal Service after walking a delivery route for 12-plus years, then working in the post office sorting room for another 12-plus years—and now self-employed as a private dick. His annual income consisted almost entirely of USPS pension benefits, while private dickwork tended to be a thankless profession.

Max checked **[X] Currently Working**, checked **[X] -40K**, and moved on.

No, he did not **Vigorously Exercise** regularly, but his **General Health** was **[X] Good** .

He had never consumed **Alcohol**, except a few times accidentally, and had never **Smoked** or indulged in use of **Recreational Drugs**.

After answering other questions related to his driving record and… What in Sam Hill? Max was startled to finally arrive at a blinking box captioned **CALCULATE My Life Expectancy.**

With a trembling finger poised inches above the computer keyboard…

Buzz. Buzz. Buzz.

…Max deferred knowing his scheduled check-out date and picked up his phone.

The call was from Doc Sanders' office. After listening for a minute or two…Oh no, looking up at a wall-mounted clock, his fate hit him like a fistful of knuckles to the kisser. The dreaded hour had come for putting his worldly affairs in order.

CHAPTER TWO

In unseasonably bearable December weather Dr. John Sanders stood on the tee box of the country club's practice range, looking down at a golf ball and trying to relax.

Whoosh!

"Damn!" Another shank. He would never post a score in even the neighborhood of his advanced age, unless…With the head of his five-iron he nudged another ball onto an undivoted spot of dead grass, stood over the ball and again tried to relax.

Whoosh!

"Damn!" What with one thing and another, he didn't get to play nearly as much as needed to finally realize his potential. Oklahoma weather was harsh-to-unpleasant at least six months of the year. One member of his regular foursome had died, another was now incapacitated by arthritis, and Mike Erwin had lost his marbles. He'd tried to interest the wife, but…

Whoosh!

"Damn!" Candice didn't like to play golf, didn't like for him to play, and was adamantly against retirement that would allow them to move to Florida. Seniors living down in Boca Grande were tanned, rested, and…

Whoosh!

"Damn!"

He too was ready, willing and still able to play golf or go out on a boat every day instead of continuing to trudge along in the same rut like a rented mule pulling a plow.

Charlie Perkins—a retired dentist and eighteen-handicapper—was down there in the Sunshine State, living the

good life with his first-and-only wife, Connie, and likely to reach a platinum age close or equal to the gross number of strokes on his daily scorecard. His lifelong friend and best man at both of his weddings had tried to...

Whoosh!

"Damn!"

Thirty-odd years ago, Charlie had tried to warn him—in the musical words of Jerry Lee Lewis—that he was "middle-aged crazy". And in fact, Doc now realized, he had been forty-odd-years-old but maybe "going on thirty/ trying to prove he still can". Candice was actually not yet thirty at the time, and Charlie...

Looking down the muddy range devoid of well-hit balls, he recalled his best man's more detailed advice, lifted from an Eighties musical revue called *Tom*—for a songwriter, Tom Lehrer—*Foolery*, and delivered at a second so-called "bachelor party". Standing on a chair with glass in hand—wearing a wig of long, straight, dark hair to suggest Candice's most distinctive feature—Charlie, in falsetto, had sung...

♫*Since I still appreciate you/ Let's find love while we may/ Because I know I will hate you/ When you are old and gray...* ♫

Whoosh!

"Damn!"

Doc nudged another ball into position and tried to clear his mind of regret, but ...

♫*While enjoying our compatibility/ I am cognizant of its fragility/ And I question the advisability/ Of relying on its durability...* ♫

Whoosh!

♫*You're aware of my inflexibility/ And my quintessential volatility/ And the total inconceivability/ Of me showing true humility...* ♫

Whoosh!

♫*Though my undeniable nubility/ May excuse a certain puerility/ Your alleged indispensability/ Underestimates my versatility...* ♫

Whoosh!

"Damnit!" Candice had never been a real "nurse", only an attractive, flirtatious receptionist and bookkeeper for his medical

practice. But now…now…Over the course of thirty years their roles relative to one another had somehow changed. Now, he had to admit, she "wore the pants"!

Whoosh!

For crying out loud, after discovering what she thought was a loophole in insurance policies, his wife and nominal subordinate had recently taken it upon herself to administer—without his approval—medical treatment of male patients for…

Whoosh!

He himself would never risk potentially lethal doses of… Realizing that the sack of balls was now empty, Doc dropped his five-iron to the barren ground.

He should have foreseen the time would come when big-city hospitals would move into the market with so-called "Doc-in-the-Box" drive-thru units such as the one newly opened on the highway east of downtown. More importantly, he should have foreseen the time would come when he would be sick-and-tired of looking into patients' mouths, probing their bellies, pretending to give a damn about their chronic complaints. And even more to the point…

♪*Your boyish irresponsibility/ And what now is charming juvenility/ Will in time lose adorability/ And appear much more like imbecility…* ♪

He should have listened to Charlie Perkins and foreseen that while he would deserve to someday take it easy and enjoy life, a younger mate, namely Candice—still concerned with having enough hay in the barn to see herself through an approaching winter season of life—would keep him in harness until he dropped, or…

♪*I'll never love you then at all/ The way I do today/ So please remember/ When I leave in December/ I told you so in May* ♪

CHAPTER THREE

After checking his safe deposit box to confirm that his last will-and-testament was in order, Max hurried from the local Last National Bank and hotfooted along Main Street in a sweat. Only a week ago he'd gotten a passing grade on a routine physical exam, but ...Only minutes ago Doc Sanders' office had called to say that a box on his chart "raised troubling issues".

What box?

Heart? He'd immediately noticed fluttering chest pains and shortness of breath.

Kidneys? Urine running down his leg onto the floor of his copy shop cubicle had felt feverish.

Head? He'd detected nothing "upstairs" except fog, but...

Rushing into the doc's storefront office..."Ah, Mr. Morgan," said the past-her-prime but still dark-haired tomato—identified by nameplate as "Candy"—who served as both Sanders' assistant and Missus. "Go into the examination room and take off your clothes."

Max did as directed and—down to nothing but socks and undies—mentally braced himself for delivery of a smarty-pants "I-told-you-so" verdict from the doc. At their most recent encounter the old sawbones—himself well past a reasonable retirement age if not expiration date—had been as rosy-cheeked as ever, but...

"Same insurance still in force?" said the medico's Missus, entering the exam room with clipboard in hand, then eyeing...

Max covered his privates area with a hand.

"You left the 'Sexually Active' box unchecked during your

recent visit, Mr. Morgan. Why?"

Oh, that box. Well, he was single, he explained. As well as, uh, getting up in age, he added in response to the dubious look in her eyes. Was wedlock to "Candy" the secret to the long-in-the-tooth doc's longevity?

"Try not to worry," she said. "Based on a more thorough diagnosis, we may be able to fix your problem. And insurance will pay for the treatment. Drop the tightie-whities and bend over."

But…But…But where was Doc Sanders?

"The doctor is out, probably playing golf," said the wife with a snort. "But again, not to worry. I am a trained nurse."

But…But…But…

"Let's put the PSA lab results to the test by digitally examining that prostate of yours," she said, putting a rubber glove onto a hand.

Prostate? OMG! Feeling weak in the knees, Max turned around, bent over as instructed, and…

"Uh hum, size of a grapefruit," the trained nurse said from behind him. "No wonder you're suffering from ED."

ED?

"Erectile Disfunction. But not to worry. An industrial-strength dose of *Mister Bones* will have you up-and-at-it in a jiffy. And it's covered by insurance."

Max felt a prick…immediately followed by a hot facial blush and…told to turn around…a hot full-body blush!

"Hmmm," the doc's wife hmmmed, again eyeing him with a dubious look in her eyes.

Max covered his exposed privates with both hands.

"I think I know just 'what the doctor ordered'," she said, undoing a button of her white uniform.

Max began to detect a strange sensation "downstairs" and…

"What in Sam Hill is going on in here," said Doc Sanders, entering the exam room with, uh oh, a golf club in hand.

"Not to worry, John," said the Missus to her red-faced spouse. "The treatment is covered by insurance and…Yes," she said, again

eyeing, "another dose ought to do the trick."

"No, Candice, absolutely not!" said the doc. "Another dose could be fatal."

Fatal?

Max again detected fluttering chest pains. Again he noticed bladder leakage, and…The next thing he knew, he was lying on the exam room floor. The next thing he heard was Doc Sanders accusing his wife of intent to commit homicide!

CHAPTER FOUR

As her doddering husband wasted time in the exam room on unbillable "consultation" with the hopelessly hypochondriacal patient—Maxwell Morgan—Candice went about the real work of running a medical practice: prepping insurance company forms for payment of an amount due for legitimate services rendered. A piddling sum in relation to the treatment she herself had provided, and a drop in the bucket toward what she would need for her Golden Years.

At almost sixty, she should already be enjoying life and looking forward to decades of leisure to come, but…Ancient wisdom contained in a book titled *The Midwife's Guide*—discovered by her, alas, too late in life—now echoed inside her head, to-wit:

When greedy parents, for the sake of riches, will match a daughter to an old man, can anyone imagine that such a conjunction can ever yield satisfaction, where the inclinations are as opposite as the months of May and December.

Yes, she blamed her old-fashioned mother for effectively pimping her into a life of servitude and ultimate poverty by pushing her to become a nurse, and for glorifying doctors as ideal mates. Oh yes, though her mother was not Jewish, and as the old joke went, had never actually yelled "Is there a doctor in the house?!"—not to summon medical help, but to introduce her daughter to a prospective groom—she had regularly expressed devout hope that her daughter would meet-and-marry a "Dr. Right".

Also alas, however, young-and-single M.D.s had no money, and John—already married with children when she went to

work "under" him—was almost fifteen years older than she. Thirty years ago, their difference in age had not seemed to matter, but divorce from a first wife who helped him through medical school had been costly, raising their own offspring had been expensive, and the generation gap between them had widened through the years in proportion to her husband's waistline and in disproportion to his bottom line.

Not to mention how increasingly tiresome their May-and-December marriage had become. Mothers of daughters had no idea how boring the domestic company of older men could be. And John was particularly afflicted with the stereotypical qualities commonly attributed to doctors.

Totally lack of good taste, for instance. Whereas the large picture of dogs playing poker might have been suitable for a basement den of sorts, his insistence that the "art" salvaged from his divorce be prominently displayed in their living room was beyond embarrassing. And white socks! Okay for the golf course, she supposed, but at cocktail parties…mortifying!

Also a total lack of…While nervous patients occasionally laughed at "doctor's" incredibly moronic golfing puns—"It takes a lot of balls to play the game," for instance—at social gatherings…No matter how many times she reminded him that the punchline for the tired old joke passed down by his father was "pasteurized", he never failed to leave listeners gaping in silent confusion when told that a famous diva took milk baths that were "heh, heh, not 'homogenized', just up to her tits!"

Worst of all, he was particularly stereotypical—like the proverbial cobbler whose own family went without shoes—in his lack of concern for loved ones closest to him, namely her! Though her mischosen mate wasted way too much time hanging out with other loafers at the golf club, not a day passed when he did not whine about wanting to retire and move to the "elephant graveyard" known as Florida, with no regard whatsoever to building instead of wasting a nest egg for the twenty-five to thirty-odd years she would likely outlive him.

This makes the woman who still wants a husband (for an old man

*is scarcely the shadow of one) either to wish, or may be, to contrive his
death, or else, to satisfy her natural inclinations, she throws herself
into the arms of unlawful love, which might have been prevented had
her inconsiderate parents provided her with a suitable match.*

Candice sighed the forlorn sigh of what might have been.

She had effectively "gifted" her worthless college boyfriend,
Larry, to a sister, Cornelia, not in her wildest dreams imagining
the feckless frat boy would go on to become a filthy rich real
estate developer in Tulsa. Corny was now happily divorced and
comfortably wealthy—clipping bond coupons to often travel
throughout the world when not lolling at her luxurious winter
home in Boca Grande, Florida—while she herself spent her
days soliciting patients and scrapping with insurance companies
for meager...

"Well, here I am," said a trembling male voice. "I had to call
for an Uber ambulance to get here for the urgent appointment
you ordered."

Candice looked across her desk and saw that an old man
confined to a wheelchair had rolled into the office's reception
area.

"Ah, yes, Mr. Wheeler, uh, Whelan," she said, reaching for a
clipboard. "Just an urgently routine follow-up to make sure you
are as comfortable as possible."

"Well, I'm still in constant pain, but under the circumstances..."

"Any falls since your last visit?"

"Yes, at least once a day."

"Any more fainting spells?"

"They're why I fall out the chair."

"Any thoughts of suicide?"

"Constantly. The doc said I have only weeks if not days to live,
but my insurance wouldn't pay if..."

"Changes to your insurance coverage since your last visit?!"

"Oh no, I keep my life insurance paid up, for my wife to live
on when..."

Interested solely in the patient's medical insurance coverage for
treatment of likely Erectile Disfunction, Candice—in reaction

to the old man's mention of providing for a widow — ground her teeth.

While her own overaged husband wasted time on the so-called "tee box" at one or another golf course, a young Pakistani so-called "Doc-in-the-Box" was now processing patients like green grass through a goose at a local drive-thru clinic. While her selfish spouse was spending money like a drunken sailor, on golf, on ugly clothes and…For crying out loud, how many clashing patterns of paisley-versus-plaids and dull-to-duller shades of tan could there be? Like Medicare outlays, no doubt the bulk of their joint savings would be expended during the last six months of his life. So yes…

She becomes impatient for her husband's death, and thinks every day an age to live with him…

"My God, Roger, what in blazes are you doing here?" said John, coming into the waiting area, as the overweight Mr. Morgan darted for a rear exit. "You should be home in bed, letting that good wife of yours make you as comfortable as possible."

…and therefore seeks opportunity to cut off that thread of life which she opines nature lengthened out too long.

Candice ignored the morbid echo. John's life was hopelessly underinsured. For her to live happily ever after, she needed her marital helpmate to keep on pulling his weight, and hers, at a more industrious, not a more "relaxed" pace.

CHAPTER FIVE

Shaken by the close call inside Doc Sanders' exam room, Max laid low in the alley behind Mister Quickie's copy shop. He needed to pick up a few things from his office — specifically including his Roscoe — before laying lower, and...Seeing that the coast was finally clear, he hotfooted to the rear entrance to the copy shop, let himself inside, ankled toward his cubicle, and . . .

Finding that the teenaged kid who served as his case report jotter had parked his big be-hind in the client chair, Max plopped into his own double-wide chair and commenced to put the kid semi-wise to what had gone down in an almost exact re-play of the final scene in Mike Hammer's most famous case.

"So the jealous husband caught you with your pants down," said the kid, "almost *en flagrante* with his Missus. And now, almost like Pops McCaffrey in Mr. Hammer's *Case of Coney Island Baby*, the old doc has it in for you. Right?"

The kid, a wannabe gumshoe, had also studied all the pulp case reports from back in the *Noir*. He also knew chapters-and-verses word-for-word, but — tending to get Hammer's lays mixed up with one another — usually got things only half right, at best.

"The doc's Missus is not the kind of dame a guy wishes he had met before," he explained to the green-as-grass wannabe. "Like Charlotte Manning in Mike's *Case of* . . . "

"Mrs. Sanders a *femme fatale*? No way, Mr. Maximo. She's got to be years older than even you."

"She's what they call a 'cougar', kid, a feline man-eater on the prowl. And — to put it in R-rated terms — what went down in the doc's exam room was a dead ringer for the ending of Mike

Hammer's *Case of I, the Jury.*"

The kid dropped his jaw, obviously shocked that sordid facts of life could be in play right there in the small town of Henryetta, Oklahoma.

"Are you saying the doc's Missus 'hooked her thumbs in the fragile silk of her undies and pulled them down'?" the babe-in-the-woods finally said. "That she came toward you 'with arms outstretched? Lightly running her tongue over her lips, making them glisten with passion and…?'"

"Well, not exactly," Max admitted. "And she didn't actually 'sigh, making the hemispheres of her breasts quiver'. But she was, almost, close enough to 'lean forward to kiss me, with her arms going out to encircle my neck' and…"

"OMG, Mr. Max, are you saying Mrs. Sanders had put a gun in a potted plant behind you, 'with the safety catch off and a silencer attached'?"

Well, there was no potted plant in the exam room, but…

"Are you saying 'those loving arms would have reached the rod nicely'? That 'a face waiting to be kissed was really waiting to be splattered with blood when she blew your head off'?"

"Well, no, not exactly. I backed away and thankfully…"

"Please, Mr. Max; please tell me you didn't plug Mrs. Sanders with your Roscoe."

"I wasn't packing heat. When the doc came into the room I, uh, laid low, and overheard him finger his Missus for attempted homicide."

"Hmmm," the kid hmmmed, leaning back in his chair. "As you yourself well know, Mr. Max, in most cases involving a married dame's hanky-panky with another man, it's the jealous husband who feels, and sometimes acts 'homicidal'."

"Listen and learn, kid," said Max, getting up from his chair. "The cougar is a man-eater scorned, homicidally furious as hell at Yours Truly! Tonight—this afternoon actually—I go to the mattress."

WEDNESDAY

December 17, 2025

CHAPTER SIX

Max again checked that the back door of the house he'd always shared with his mom was securely double-locked, then returned to the kitchen table for a second batch of scrambled eggs, bacon, and a cinnamon rolls.

Following yesterday's close call with the man-eating cougar, he'd forgotten to check the high-tech "crystal ball" box labeled **CALCULATE My Life Expectancy**, which was just as well. As a private dick—the kind of guy that *femme fatales* such as Candy Sanders were drawn to like moths—the genie inside the computer would probably have added up a "buy-by" date for Yours Truly of only...

"Max, I know Mrs. Sanders," Mom again said as she re-filled his coffee cup, "and I know you. On both counts, I think it highly unlikely that she 'staged an intimate physical examination' and 'drugged' you with intent to get 'frisky'. As for 'undressing', I feel quite certain she must have been idly fidgeting with a button of her nurse's uniform while lost in thought about something."

Yeah, sure, and Jackie Kennedy was not involved in the rub-out of JFK by the Greek goombah she went on to bed-and-wed.

Mom was also dubious that the doc's Missus would be "homicidal"—especially toward him in particular—even though Charlotte Manning had tried to blow Mike Hammer's head off in *Case of I, the Jury*, even though Brigid O'Shaughnessy had knocked off Sam Spade's partner in *Case of the Maltese Falcon*, and would have done the same to Sam if he'd not wised-up to her game. Not to mention that in *Case of Double Indemnity* another *femme fatale*, Phyllis Dietrichson, had sweet-talked an

insurance salesman to deep-six her husband in order to collect...

Hmmm.

He'd been enveloped in haze while lying on Doc Sanders' exam room floor. And now that he re-noodled the near-death experience with a clear head...

Hmmm.

Sanders and his Missus had got into a spat about her giving Yours Truly a possibly fatal dose of *Mister Bones* alright, but had gone on to squabble more heatedly about the doc's waste of time on golf versus the wife's determination to keep <u>him</u> at the grindstone that..."bordered on homicidal". In other words, what a relief!

Hmmm.

Case of She Just Snapped came to mind, one of hundreds documented on the *True Crime Channel* that he had worked with Mom through the years, almost all of which involved dames putting spouses permanently "out to and under grassy pastures".

Hmmm.

Max reminded his mom of the *Snapped* case in which a Mrs. Schreiner called 911 to frantically report that her husband of more than forty years appeared to have dropped dead in the driveway of their cozy residence. The bloody scene, however, indicated not a routine fall, but murrrderrr. Based on reports of a longstanding quarrel with a neighbor, cops grilled the identified suspect and, bingo.

Though 77, the neighbor copped to carrying on an affair with the 71-year-old Mrs. Schneider.

"Elderly people need, and are capable of engaging in, uh, affection," said his 75-year-old mom. "And at her trial, the, uh, widow in the Schneider case testified that her ailing husband had been impatient with her, yelled at her, watched her because she didn't always do what he wanted right away. And told that the mental abuse got worse as he got older."

Yeah, so the old broad fed her husband a dose of drugs called *Ambien* and sent him out to play tennis. When that didn't stop his ticker...

"She should have known *Ambien* and exercise would not, uh, do the trick," said Mom. "Mrs. Schneider was a nurse, after all."

Bingo.

Doc Sanders' Missus was also a trained nurse, so…Yeah, after years of being caged in wedlock to the doc, the man-eating cougar was homicidal alright, not with having Yours Truly in mind for "lunch", but—already fed up with her spouse—likely to "just snap" at any minute!

CHAPTER SEVEN

Doc imagined himself standing at the top of a high pedestal, which did not seem out of order. From beneath, a covey of women dressed in white looked up to him, each holding in her hands a bunch of grapes.

"*Yes, doctor*," said one.

"*Yes, doctor*," said another.

"*Yes, doctor*," said a third.

"*Yes.*"

"*Yes.*"

"*Yes.*"

An adoring dark-haired damsel stood out from the covey of nurses. Candice, still fresh as a garden flower, holding in her hands...

"*No!*" he thundered.

"*No!*" he repeated.

"*No!*" Doses of *Mister Bones* were not to be administered to anyone except himself!

A lei of artificial carnations dropped from around Candice's neck...She began to unbutton her pristine uniform... turned away and moved toward a naked...Max Morgan?

Doc woke with a start. Staring at his feet propped up in front of him, he realized he was lying on his back in the large recliner inside the knotty pine-paneled den of his—and Candice's—house. A mantel clock illuminated by bright daylight coming through a window informed him it was mid-morning. What in blazes?

Oh yeah, now he recalled storming out of the office yesterday afternoon...returning to the country club practice range to again

flail at balls…joining some acquaintances in the men's lounge for a few hands of gin rummy and…returning home to find the door to the master bedroom locked.

Damnit, gin always caused nightmares, but. . . Max Morgan? The overweight ex-mailman who now fancied himself a "private dick" was a bumbling fool., and… For crying out loud, yesterday's spat with Candice was solely about her administering erectile disfunction treatment to a patient without his prior medical approval, which—for a morbidly obese middle-aged male—could have been fatal. Morgan's ridiculous explanation—"mistaken appearance of *en fragrante delicto*"-- had been laughable, literally. He had taken it—and the fatso himself—as a joke.

Femme fatale? Ha! Candice was about to turn sixty and… Yes, with the help of regular yoga she had maintained a slender figure, and with the help of regular beauty shop "treatments" had kept her hair dark, but…

"Sixty is the new forty," his "mature" spouse had taken to repeatedly saying, almost as a mantra, "so I think of myself as still in my thirties."

For Candice to undertake examination, if not treatment of a patient in his absence was not unusual, but…For her to have supposedly told Morgan to strip "undies and all" was… inappropriate under the circumstances. And…And…And now that he thought about it, though difficult to make out under his drooping belly—and iffy in both size and angle—did the patient have an erection when "caught en *fragrante*"?

Doc dismissed the grotesque imagery from his mind, or rather tried to. Though he and his wife of thirty years had been squabbling of late, though she had taken to making references to their age difference …Max Morgan? Impossible.

On the other hand, the ex-mailman, though about fifty, had a certain almost "boyish" youthful look. Never married and divorced, his no doubt generous tax payer-funded postal service pension would be unencumbered. As for his current fanciful vocation as a "private dick", hell, even intelligent women, he'd

been told, were avid readers of so-called "detective stories". And Candice in particular—not very smart—was a devoted fan of the portly PBS "sleuth", Father Brown.

Hmmm.

But no, not Max Morgan. The fat man's appearance in a nightmare was only...

"Never waste jealousy on a real man," he recalled someone famously saying. "It is the 'imaginary man' that supplants us all in the long run." And of course he had also heard the famous line that jealousy was a "green-eyed monster that "mocks the meat it feeds on." True for all ordinary men perhaps, but he was a doctor, intelligently above such feelings of insecurity.

On the other hand...His longtime wife thinking of herself as "still thirty" brought to mind onset of his own drawn out —though long past --so-called "midlife crisis", during which his friend, Charlie Perkins, had diagnosed him as crazy as a...

Ding Dong.

Doc pulled a lever to launch himself from the recliner. Still dressed in yesterday's golfing clothes, he went to the front door, opened it, and...Oh no, there stood the unimagined "other" man in the flesh, Max Morgan!

"Note on the office door said you were under the weather," said the obese patient, "so dropped by to continue our man-to-man chat about the, uh, delicate situation."

Delicate situation? Stunned, but determined not to show signs of caring that would give Morgan—and Candice—satisfaction...

"What are your intentions?" Doc managed to say.

"I'll keep an eye on the box of 'candy' in your absence."

The homewrecker made it sound like he was doing him, the pathetic, uh, "cuckold", a favor by...What brass!

"I myself have no intention of leaving this house, ever!"

"Better for you to get out of the line-of-fire, Doc. More often than not, these love triangles lead to murrrderrr."

Murrrderrr?

"Are you threatening me, Morgan?"

"Just professional-to-professional advice, Doc. To avoid risk of getting the rubber-glove treatment from the Missus, better make yourself scarce until Yours Truly identifies a next patsy the frisky *femme* tries to sucker into her honey pot."

Next patsy?

"Hourly charge, plus expenses, due and payable only if you survive. Which reminds me: to eliminate the usual motive, better cancel any life insurance you have in play."

To his relief, somewhat, Doc realized that the fat man was "chatting man-to-man" as a "private dick", not necessarily as a...a romantic rival, but... Suggestion that his services were called for was absurd, but...Despite himself—a doctor!—the idea of Candice having a "next patsy" dipping into her "honey pot" was maddening.

CHAPTER EIGHT

After stripping down to his undies, Max commenced to don a disguise composed of materials he had spread out on his bed: brassiere, stuffed with wadded-up socks...his mom's loose-fitting dress, and a pair of her shoes...handbag...granny glasses...and straight black-haired wig from an old Three Stooges party game, tied down by a calico scarf.

He looked into a mirror. Perfect. The mark would never suspect she was being tailed by a good-looking middle-aged broad.

Passing through the kitchen on his way out, he noticed a stack of books that Mom must have left lying on a counter:

Love Never Ages, A Seniors' Guide to Dating...

How to Not Die Alone, The Surprising Science That Will Help You Find Love ...

To serve as a prop for looking occupied while on a stakeout in a public place, he picked up a hardback titled *Single, Shy and Looking for Love*, then ankled from the house.

Fifteen minutes later—posted on the Main Street sidewalk across the street from where Doc Sanders and the Missus headquartered—he waited for an unsuspecting "fly" to enter the the black widow spider's "parlor". Yeah, ordinary Joes-and-Janes thought private dicking was all wine, women and song, punctuated by exciting bouts of rough stuff in back alleys. In fact, savvy dickwork involved a lot of down time...

"Those bangs need a trim job, Max," said Fred Austin, now retired but still in the habit of sitting on a bench out front of his former barber shop.

...for noodling tricky situations and plotting next moves to off-set twists of plots that might come up.

"Max, would you please tell your mother to call me as soon as possible," said Lena Austin, a manicurist, after coming out of the shop. "I have some new nail colors she might like for her toes."

The Doc's Missus—having struck out with Yours Truly yesterday—had likely set up a second-string patsy to come in for the old prostate-exam tease and a shot of *Mister Bones*. Probably she was now unbuttoning her nursing blouse. Within minutes, the flirtatious skirt would likely fade the office, headed for a lunchtime tryst at the no-tell motel on the western <u>out</u>skirts of town. He would tail her and...

"How they hangin', Max?" said a passer-by as... Bingo, Candy Sanders came out onto the sidewalk across the street and ankled toward 12th Street, where—two steps ahead—he had parked Mom's brown Buick boiler. But...

After crossing 10th Street, the deadly dame ducked into a joint called Tillie's Tea Room, a new, no doubt dimly lit dive for illicit rendezvous. Her juiced-up hot-to-trot patsy would no doubt be joining her by way of a back alley. Yours Truly would relocate the stakeout and...

"Hey, 'Sherlock', what's with the dress?" said J.J. Coates, loitering as usual outside his so-called field services office. "In disguise for a 'stakeout'? Haw, Haw, Haw."

Noting that his cover must have come undone, Max tidied the scarf and wig before entering into what turned out to be a brightly lit tea room, where...

"Will you be dining alone?" said a middle-aged broad at the front. "Or are you expecting to be joined?"

Max eased his double-wide backside onto an uncomfortably small chair at an also dainty table, took the book from Mom's handbag, and—while doping out the tea room twist—pretended to read. Yeah, "hiding in plain sight" was the oldest trick in the book for double-dealing married dames and...

Hmmm.

Another broad—probably a "beard" for double-cover—came

to the cagey *femme fatale's* table, sat down, and… "So glad you called," he heard her say. "What are sisters for, if not to be there in times of crisis."

♫*Sisters, sisters…* ♫

An old song from an old movie…

There were never such devoted sisters… ♫

…came to mind, and …

♫*Two different faces, but in tight places/ we think and act as one…* ♫

As he continued to eavesdrop, Max doped out that the Doc's Missus had confided marital dissatisfaction and financial worries to the sibling named Cornelia, who semi-sympathetically said: "I told you so, Candy. I warned you not to marry an older man, and a doctor at that."

♫*Many men have tried to split us up/ but no one can…* ♫

"Bullshit, Corny, you were green with envy when John escaped your clutches and fell into mine."

"We were both young, both anxious to be Mother's favorite, and…"

♫*Lord help the mister/ who comes between me and my sister…* ♫

"And horny in your case, Sister. For God's sake, you tried to screw him 'under the table', not 'so to speak', at our wedding rehearsal dinner."

"I thought I was in love, Candy. And in 'my case', unlike yours, it wasn't just social and financial ambition that attracted me to 'Dr. Right'."

"I was pregnant, for Christsake. I had no choice."

"Yeah, sure, you made a 'mistake'. But it's not too late to…"

"Me too," said a semi-elderly joker, seating himself at Max's table, then picking up the book that lay there. "*Single, Shy, and Looking for Love*," he announced, before opening the *Dating Guide for the Shy and Socially Anxious* and commencing to read aloud an Introduction of sorts:

"'What if he thinks I'm not good looking enough? What is she thinks I'm boring?'"

Max played it cool as the would-be masher scanned the page.

"Ah, yes, "'Confidence is the most attractive quality a man or woman can have…If you're ready to stop being a wallflower and start putting out'…oops, 'start putting yourself out there…'"

"Beat it, Buster," Max growled. "I'm too…You're too old to handle a broad like Yours Truly."

As the disappointed pick-up artist scurried from the tea room…

"I'm only trying to be helpful, Candice," said the sister, getting up from the other table in what looked to be also a huff. "It's your second and last chance to make a right 'choice'. Get rid of him before he runs off to Florida with all the money!"

♫*And Lord help the sister/ that comes between me and my man…*♫

Yeah, like every private dick from Henryetta to Hoboken, he'd heard this song before, Max more clearly doped out. No doubt the Doc's Missus --- if not stopped from "getting rid of" her Mister—would later claim her wicked sister had put her up to the dirty deed.

CHAPTER NINE

Struggling to maintain an outward appearance of cool while seething inside, Candice nibbled a cucumber sandwich. She might have turned a blind eye to John spending yesterday morning <u>and</u> afternoon <u>and</u> evening at the club... playing golf, playing cards and drinking martinis...missing dinner and getting home quite late...waking no doubt in a hung-over pout and failing to make it into the office this morning...but she would not forgive-and-forget her husband siccing on her the oafish so-called private detective now sitting across the small tea room, ridiculously "disguised" as...

Why would John do such a thing? What had the old fool been told by the obese patient during yesterday's post-treatment "consultation"? While suspicious jealousy was said by some to be a sign of passionate love—indeed, that a man's love could be measured by the jealousy that came with it—surely her husband of almost thirty-years would not think he had walked in on... The very thought of any such suspicion was as absurd as it was revolting. And John's passion for anything other than golf had dibbled down into his shoes long ago. Their life together had become...

♫Every day a little death/ In the parlor, in the bed/ In the buttons and the bread... ♫

Yes, like the Count and Countess in the famous musical play, *A Little Night Music...*

♫Every move and every breath/ And you hardly feel a thing/ Brings a perfect little death... ♫

Candice identified with Countess Charlotte, married to a

vain and arrogant buffoon with ego large and fragile as a blimp. Uncaring about anyone but himself, unseeing that... Criminy, with dark black bangs hanging from a cleaning woman's scarf 'round his head, Maxwell Morgan looked like the oldtime so-called slapstick comedian, What's-His-Name, Joe...? No, "Moe" Somebody.

Hmmm.

In an effort to prick her "blimp", Countess Charlotte had made a show of throwing herself at an attractive younger man named Frederic. And it worked. Her previously indifferent husband became a possessive "tiger" and challenged her fake lover to a duel of Russian roulette.

Hmmm.

The idea of spitefully provoking a neglectful spouse's jealousy was not so fanciful as to be unbelievable. From a nursing school Psychology class of not so long ago, Candice recalled a professor's lecture about "mate-choice copying": a principle derived from observation that members of various species were inclined to find potential mates desirable if they saw that others did, possibly explaining why some crafty human females wore fake wedding rings for bar outings.

And essentially the same phenomenon was reportedly seen in sexually jaded South American monkeys, one male specimen of which regained interest in his mate only after zoo keepers rigged a stereo near their enclosure and played pre-recorded mating calls of other males.

Hmmm.

So yes, John might be susceptible to a dose of his own medicine, but...Looking across the tea room at Max Morgan... No, much as she would relish avenging her mate's disgusting insult, she could not bring herself to even imagine stooping to...

♫*I'm before him on my knees/ He assumes I'll lose all reason/ And I do...* ♫

Candice retrieved her phone from her handbag and punched in a number. In a slightly raised voice...

"Ari, darling," she said to her handsome young hairdresser.

"Wonderful news: My aged husband is under the weather and…
Yes, possibly a bout with gout," she said with a giggle. "So I might
as well close the office for the afternoon, and…

"Yes, exactly what I had in mind, tee hee…

"Oh yes, the 'full monty', tee hee…But, darling, I must be
back home by dark in case John…

"I know, I know, my sister just now told me I should get rid
of him, but…

"Your place in thirty minutes," she announced, and with
phone still to her ear after discreetly turning it off: "We'll bill-
and-coo about a next move then, in bed. Ta-ta, my love."

As she passed by the private dickhead's table on her way out, he
lowered his head, maybe or maybe not pretending to examine his
tiny tea room sandwich in search of, say, a pork chop. Hopefully,
the gumshoe would "tail" her to her hair appointment and also
fail to detect that Ari—though good-looking and physically
prime as a Greek god—was flamboyantly gay.

Yes, to "make a monkey" of John was a dirty trick, but she
was hardly the first "devious" female to use the ploy. In a famous
old English novel she'd been made to read in high school, the
heroine—Jane Eyre—purposefully used another man to induce
jealousy in her true love. In *The Empire Strikes Back*, Princess
Leia made a show of kissing Luke on the lips for the "cynical"
purpose of inflaming jealousy in Han. Virtually every girl in
every teeny-bopper drama ever made, from *Beach Blanket Bingo*
to *Grease*, staged fake romances to pierce the egos of immature
males, but…

♫*Ooh, I wanna dance and sing/ Politics, not my thing/ Ooh
but then I met the king/ And soon my daddy said/ "Don't lose your
head."*…♫

True, the tactic didn't work for the teenaged Scarlett, who
went so far as to marry another man in a vain, petulant attempt
to rouse jealous passion in Ashley Wilkes, but…

♫*Sorry, not sorry 'bout what I said/ I'm just tryin' to have some
fun*…♫

Back at the medical office to clear the appointments docket,

Candice realized the song that had popped into her head was not about Scarlett O'Hara's failed gambit, nor was it about Countess Charlotte's success in *A Little Night Music*. It was from another touring Broadway play she had attended in Tulsa — titled *Six* — sung by the doomed heroine, Anne Boleyn, in a failed attempt to explain away her alleged infidelities as staged appearances intended to make her husband jealous.

♫*Don't worry, don't worry, don't lose your head/ I didn't mean to hurt anyone . .* ♫

CHAPTER TEN

Max brought the brown boiler to a stop out front of a red-brick building on the southern outskirts of town. Told by a uniformed flunky that "help" was required to park out back, he stated his business: to have an urgently helpful word or two with Doc Sanders, who — according to a housemaid — would likely be found at the country club.

He had tailed the doc's devious Missus from the tea room to the medical office and then to the nearby town of Okmulgee. There, he had eyeballed the cougar creeping into a joint fronted by a mirrored sign as *Missus Narcissus Beauty Salon*. Yeah, sure, for a "full monty" that would curl her hair and put roses in her cheeks. Now back to home base with the goods on the frisky *femme*...

By the flunky's pointed finger, Max's attention was directed toward a nearby "range" — unoccupied by horses and cows — where a couple of guys and a doll were digging up clumps of sod with what looked to be...

Yeah, they were swinging golf clubs, he noted, after ankling across a paved parking lot onto the "range" and approaching...

Whoosh!

"Damn!"

In his disguise as a broad, he had rung a salon doorbell, but — greeted by way of a speaker and sized-up through a peep hole — was told that "R.E." didn't do "dos" for hopeless cases. Afterward however, he had canvassed the surrounding neighborhood of shops and found out...

Whoosh!

"Damn!"

As the client lined up for another whoosh…

"Sorry to interrupt your afternoon relaxation, Doc, but for your safety you need to know without delay…"

Whoosh!

"Damn!"

"…I tailed the, uh, 'lady in question' to an out-of-town 'appointment'," Max reported in a lowered voice. "At this very moment she's getting 'doed' by…"

"What the hell?" said the startled doc. "Is…Is that you, Morgan? You and your muckraked…muck are not welcome on the range."

Yeah, same old story: kill the messenger of unglad tidings. One of the reasons savvy gumshoes usually shied away from lays leading to marital Splitsville was that clients tended to be ungrateful for the awful truth dug up by private dicks.

Whoosh!

"Damn!"

Like forcing down a dose of epsom salts for the doc's own welfare…

Whoosh!

"Damn!"

"At this very moment the Missus is playing side-pocket pool in an Okmulgee love nest with her boy toy," Max reported.

With the doc's attention knocked off the ball at his feet …

"Boy toy?"

"Young dude named R.E. Ariti, said to be .. "

"How young?"

"Thirtyish, according to witnesses in the neighborhood, and …"

"Thirtyish!"

"…handsome and 'buffed up' as a Greek god, in the words of a dame minding a next-door shop. Dude's a hairdresser by trade."

"Hairdresser! The…The young…The young Greek…The young Greek 'god' is…is…is just a hairdresser!" the now red-in-the-face doc sputtered before raising his golf club above his head

and…uh oh…snapping its iron shaft with his bare hands.

As Max backed away…

"What's wrong, John?" said the range dame after rushing to the scene. "Is this, uh, woman bothering you?"

Bingo. The broad butting into the man-to-man chat was none other than the also dark-haired, almost lookalike sister he'd spotted with the doc's Missus at the tea room.

Standing there with drooped shoulders, half a golf club shaft dangling from each hand, as if in a daze…

"Candice and…and a…a…a hairdresser named R.E. Somebody," the client mumbled. "They're playing dirty pool behind my back."

"'R .E.'? You mean 'Ari' at the Missus Narcissus Salon?" said the *femme fatale's* sister, also obviously in shock. "Are you kidding? Ari is a flaming young…Uh, he's hot alright, cute in the face and buffed to the nines," she said, after seeming to have checked herself in mid-sentence. "And John, as you yourself would well know, Candy has always flaunted her long, dark hair for, uh, seduction."

"But…But…But I am a doctor," the doc wailed.

"Yes, and Candy never deserved one," said the sister, moving closer to the poor sap's side and sympathetically linking an arm in his.

"I never asked you to . . to expose…. Get off the range, Morgan!"

"She's obviously not even a member of the club!" the sister added.

With a sigh, Max turned away. Private dicking was a thankless profession alright. Often as not, duped victims of spousal double-crosses would rather let sleeping dogs lie than be put wise to awful truth. So yeah, it was the helping hands of private dicks that usually got bit, so to speak.

THURSDAY

December 20, 2025

CHAPTER ELEVEN

With the kid parked in the client chair across from him, jotting case report notes, Max leaned back in his double-wide chair, put his feet on the desk between them, and concluded his account of the lay he had titled *Case of Dickwork Outside the Box*.

"*'Outside the Box*?" said the clueless teenager, looking up with a question mark on his kisser.

"Solving a murrrderrr mystery after the fact is cake. Solving a murrrderrr mystery in advance of the deed going down is a hard-to-cook souffle that takes, savvy thinking, heh, heh, 'outside Betty Crocker's box'," Max explained.

"Take Doc Sanders, a good egg but getting up in years. Mix with stale marriage to a still saucy younger *femme fatale*. Add a sprinkle of s-e-x with a 'buttered-up' young hairdresser, and let simmer. In other words…"

"I think the term would be 'buffed-up hairdresser', Mr. Max."

"Yeah, whatever. The point is that I doped out an unusually complicated set-up for murrrderrr: older and settled-down husband…dissatisfied and still on-the-make wife… handy fall guy to do the wet work. Bingo. Doc Sanders would likely be cooled to below room temperature by now if Yours Truly had not boxed out the cougar."

"Yeah, that would fit the, uh, not completely unusual situation of, say, *Case of Double Indemnity*…*Case of The Postman Always Rings Twice*…*Case of Scarlet Street* …cases of at least half the documented murrrderrr mysteries from back in the *Noir*, but… Gee, I dunno," said the kid, still holding onto his pencil like there was more to jot. "I'm not saying you jumped to a…a possibly

wrong conclusion, Mr. Max, but you kinda hunched in a hurry that Mrs. Sanders was a 'cougar on the prowl'."

"Listen and learn, kid. When the doc's Missus made that undo-the-button move right out of Hammer's *Case of I, the Jury*, I knew I was looking into the muzzle of a loaded *femme fatale*. Took some tricky dickwork, but the doc…"

"Sometimes jealous husbands themselves react murrrderrrously after finding out…"

"…will swallow the awful truth once the shock wears off."

"Hmmm," the kid hmmmed. "In a way, your case brings to mind Mr. Sherlock's *Case of the Cardboard Box*, jotted by Doctor Watson and published in memoirs titled *His Last Bow*."

"Never heard of it," said Max, annoyed by the change of subject, then more annoyed when the bookish kid went on to irrelevantly tell that the dimwitted Scotland Yard flatfoot called Inspector Lestrade had referred to Holmes a mysterious matter of a broad receiving by mail a cardboard box—addressed to a sister who had recently moved out—containing two freshly severed human ears packed in coarse salt.

As a former mailman himself, Max was dubious that a postal worker would have unknowingly become involved in abetting an obviously nefarious scheme. He himself had always made a point to sneak a peek into cardboard boxes before passing them on.

"Other Scotland Yard detectives suspected a prank staged by medical students the woman had also recently evicted from her boarding house, but …"

"Probably the do-nutters were right for once," Max opined. "Medical students are notorious for being oddballs, which is the main reason mothers have always advised daughters not to marry doctors. In Yours Truly's case, for instance, the doc's Missus must have got sick-and-tired of him dissecting mice in the lab, cutting off ears and bringing home boring, heh, heh, 'tails'."

"Maybe so in most cases, Mr. Max, but in *Case of the Cardboard Box*, Mr. Sherlock immediately deduced, one, that medical students with access to lab chemicals would have used something better than salt to preserve the ears… two, that

medical lab students equipped with scalpels would have been able to make cleaner cuts than indicated by the ears evidence... and three, that the crudely written and partly misspelled address on the box indicated that the sender lacked education."

"Medical students are not the only types who play pranks," Max, pointed out. "It could have been neighborhood teenagers who..."

"Mr. Sherlock almost immediately suspected murrrderrr, and..."

"Murrrderrr? By ear assault?! No way."

"...went to see one of two sisters of the woman who got the box, and..."

"Let me guess. The sister was missing her ears."

"...was told by a doctor that the famous detective could not see the sister because she was suffering from 'brain fever' brought on by psychological trauma."

"Bingo! Obviously the doc had cut off the sister's ears in an ill advised attempt to cure her of an ache. Sawbones are always quick to perform profitable surgery in cases of . . ."

"No, but Mr. Sherlock found out that a third sister and her extramarital lover had recently been in fact murrrderrred. He had the bodies dug up and, bingo, inside the coffin . . ."

"Bingo?"

"Mr. Sherlock put two-and-two together, doped out that the third sister's jealous, brutish husband was the killer who had cut off his unfaithful wife's ear along with an ear of her illicit lover and put them in the box, intending for the second sister to receive and be horrified by the gory contents."

"Why?"

"Because he blamed the sister for stirring up trouble in his marriage."

"How?"

"By encouraging her sister to get involved with another man, and get rid of her brutish husband."

Hmmm.

Yeah, he'd overheard Candice Sanders' female sibling advise

her to "get rid of" the doc, Max recalled, but…Meddling? No way, José. There was no evidence that the sister in his case had sicced the hungry cougar on the Greek salon keeper, or even knew about the extramarital hanky-panky.

"You yourself passed on the suspected skinny to Mrs. Sanders' husband," Mr. Max. "And may have provoked him to…"

Max's first instinctive reaction was to clap his hands onto his own ears, but…In deafening silence, he realized the kid's wagging tongue must be blaming Yours Truly for putting the doc's wife and a young R.E. Ariti in danger, by homicidally siccing the doc on his, uh, possibly unfaithful spouse and her possibly romantic hairdoer.

CHAPTER TWELVE

Doc Sanders shuffled into Mister Quickie's copy shop, asked Tom Quickie for directions, and hobbled toward a row of workstation cubicles, where...Met with a terrified look in the eyes of Max Morgan, he put the cardboard box he carried onto the so-called private detective's desk and...

"Don't be alarmed, Morgan," he said, sitting down. "I am not the proverbial pathetically jealous husband, here to 'kill the messenger'."

In response to the fat man's wide-eyed, possibly dubious silence, he felt somehow compelled to further explain that whereas jealousy was known to be based on deep-seated personal insecurity, he was a doctor. Narcissistic, yes. Like the handsome young man of myth, he had seen his reflection in pool of water, so to speak, and liked what he saw. In other words, he was — like all successful men — proudly egosyntonic, which, in layman's terms, was to say that his behaviors, values and feelings were in no way inconsistent with his — some might enviously say — idealized self-image.

"I am a doctor," he repeated, "often distracted by weighty concerns that would crush the shoulders of lesser men, and... In a moment of stress, it was a silly aberration for me to imagine that Candice would...or ever could...with a man such as..."

With the fat man's stare still fixated on the cardboard box, Doc straightened himself. Getting to the point of his "house call"...

"I came by to, uh, 'make amends' for insanely suspecting that any wife of mine could ever...with you...And to, well, not 'thank

you', but...

"I am a doctor, and have long known that Candice—without a shred of self awareness—was always what we call 'egodytonic', which is to say that from the outset of our...our relationship, she displayed, not healthy Narcissism, but unhealthy NPD, otherwise know as 'Narcissistic Personality Disorder'.

"Somewhat, uh, younger, and coming from rather modest circumstances, her feelings of worthlessness, shame, even self-loathing were immediately apparent to me, a doctor.

"With only some nursing instruction to her credit, she is prone to compensate for her inferiority complex with cringe-worthy bragging about imagined professional skills and accomplishments. Being a social nobody prior to wedding me, a doctor, she exaggerates the degree of intimacy she enjoys with people of prominence and...

"What I mean to say is that Candice was conditioned to become, to put it kindly, a 'fabulist', severely prone to indulge in fantasies of brilliance, social standing and idealized, uh, relationships...but insecure, in need of constant and excessive expressions of, uh, admiration and...and...

"Obsessive ambition typifies sufferers of NPD. Being interpersonally exploitive is also...I wasn't fooled when she—sensing that I myself was going through a, uh, difficult period during my forties—made a play for my affections. I am a doctor, and . . .

"Anyway, I suppose I should thank you for, uh, nudging me to clearly see..."

"What's in the box?" said the self-described "gumshoe", still eyeing the cardboard container as though it might contain a bomb. Thus reminded to get to the point . . .

"Oh yeah," said Doc. "Candice had a storage room at the office cleaned-out a few months ago, to make room for her exercise bike...her yoga mat...and full-length mirrors on every wall. I took home some old files—happening to include your heath records—put them in the attic. Brought them by in case they're needed when I am, uh, gone."

"Gone?"

He was gratified by the still-frightened look in the eyes of his longtime patient who, among many others, would desperately miss him when left to impersonal Doc-in-a-Box treatment. He was not gratified, however, to then recall that Candice had also needed him, but…As the years went by and the time approached when he would need her TLC…How could any woman in her right mind opt for a…for a <u>hairdresser</u> in preference to…?

Doc got up from the chair. Once upon a time, people said he and Candice were a perfectly suited couple, but now…now people would say he had always been too good for her! Damnit, he was a doctor!

CHAPTER THIRTEEN

After tactically retreating from Doc Sanders' intended vengeance, Max—now two hours later—again sat at his desk, again warily eyeballing the still unopened box the doc had delivered. Old health records? Yeah sure, along with a deed to the Brooklyn Bridge.

Hmmm.

Contents of the container were, no doubt, intended to get back at him for telling awful truth. According to buddies still on active duty with the U.S. Postal Service, a newish medically-related outfit called *Colonguard* had made peeking into parcels or—not to mention, sniffing contents—a dicey proposition.

Hmmm.

In approximately the same vein, the box might contain a red herring, so to speak, intended to throw him off a scent of something foul still afoot.

Hmmm.

At home for lunch, Max had dug into his own files, read the case report for Sherlock Holmes' *Case of the Cardboard Box*, and yeah, the kid's hunch—though not deserving a cigar, so to speak—was in some ways close to circumstances of the case at hand. Not that Yours Truly was to blame for allegedly playing the role of a "meddlesome sister" who made a sibling's brutish husband insanely jealous by telling tales about an "other man", but...

Max had no patience for the famous British detective's braggadocio about his so-called powers of deduction. Yeah, "no shit, Sherlock", one of the ears in Holmes' case was sunburned,

so likely that of a man...and the other one matched the ears of the three sisters in a photograph displayed in plain sight... making it a walk in the park for the "master P.I." to conclude a third sister and her lover had been murrrderred.

As for all the irrelevant details put down by the case report jotter, Doc Watson, what did it matter, for instance, that the weather was hot when it all went down?

Thankfully, however, the case account was short—only twenty pages—making it digestible to readers with short attention spans, especially after a square meal followed by a nap. Even so... For crying out loud, Holmes didn't really solve the case. Not until the bumbling Inspector Lestrade found the brutish husband's written confession did the supposedly brilliant British gumshoe himself "deduct"—or would an average reader have had an inkling of—the deeper "why" of what was hardly a "whodunnit".

Yeah, the brutish husband himself had doped out that the meddlesome sister meddled because her nose was out of joint after making a play for him and getting a cold shoulder, a fact not mentioned by the clueless kid.

Hmmm?

CHAPTER FOURTEEN

Florida?!

Candice dragged her tardy husband into the medical office's exam room and held out to him his starched white jacket.

"Yeah, yeah, yeah, maybe someday, John," she shouted, "but in the meantime…For crying out loud, did you not notice the four elderly patients waiting for you to do your duty. I had to cancel the morning docket again, thanks to…"

"I'm sure you are quite capable of diagnosing and tending to their likely ailments, my dear," he answered. "You are a nurse and, I gather, rather enjoy making digital exams of prostates."

So that was why her silly husband had not come home last night. If not so annoyed, Candice would have been relieved, but…

"What did that fat fool say that brought on this childish… How dare you hire a so-called 'private detective" to snoop on me!"

"I didn't 'hire' him, Candice. I am a doctor, without time or inclination to care about your…your pathetic peccadillos. Morgan took it upon himself—he's not a doctor—to 'snoop' on you and your patsy."

"'Patsy'? You mean 'pansy'? Are you referring to my 'peccadillo' with Ari at the Missus Narcissus Salon? Ha! Have you not happened to notice that I got six inches of hair cut off?"

Silence.

"No, I thought not."

"Have you not happened to notice that I am now a blonde?"

Silence.

"No, I thought not."

"The condition of that hot buffed up patsy's prostate is of no concern to me. I am not his…"

"I know, John, but you are _my_ doctor," said Candace, changing tactics. "And you have never been more, uh, endearing to me than now. Don't you see? I was mad about…about that nosy fat man. I used him—and Ari, who happens to be, yes, 'buffed', 'hot', probably 'well endowed', but totally gay—to make you jealous. Like Countess Charlotte in _A Little Night Music_, I dangled the possibility of an 'other man' wooing me in order to make you realize …"

Assuming the old fool was embarrassed to have been made to look like, uh, an old fool, Candice would have dropped the matter, but then…

"I must assume that you, a 'nurse', have read the studies about mate retention strategies dependent on susceptibility of ordinary men to perceive a rival as superior in areas critical to self esteem," her still puffed-up mate said with a smirk. "In case you haven't noticed, my dear, I am…"

"I know John. You are…not an ordinary man. And I know you felt abandoned by your mother when she 'left you' to go to work at a cafeteria. I know the school bus often passed by without picking you up. And I know it must be, uh, stressful at times for you to be an, uh, older man, married to, uh, me. I know you are particularly, uh, 'sensitive' to pricks…"

"I am a doctor, Candice."

"I know. You took the Hippocratic Oath to bring into this exam room those patients out there, and to put on a rubber glove if necessary to meet insurance requirements for payment."

"Maybe for richer or poorer, Candice, but no, an oath of 'til death does us part is unreasonable."

"That's not the Hippocratic Oath, John. That's…"

"I know."

"Oh no."

"Candice, I am retiring to Florida as of today, with Cornelia."

"Cornelia? My sister, Cornelia? My five-years-younger than

me sister?! Cornelia, my meddling sister, who constantly tells me you're not good enough for me…"

"We have a lot in common, including golf and…"

"…and has always urged me to get rid of you!"

"…will make a perfect twosome, she says."

Hmmm.

Unlike Countess Charlotte's blimpish husband in *A Little Night Music*—driven by reawakened love to become a passionate "tiger"—her own aged spouse's umbrage was a measure of only his love of himself, Candice realized. Changing tactics again…

"Did that little tattle-tale spill the beans about me and Charlie Perkins?"

"You and Charlie?"

"You heard me."

"My God, Candice! Charlie may have an eighteen handicap, but is only a dentist! Not a jolly fellow well met who can tell a joke, and totally lacking…For crying out loud, Charlie Perkins wore a tuxedo and boring black bowtie at our rehearsal dinner. He's at least an inch shorter and in both height and…"

"And though a dentist, technically a doctor," she pointed out.

"Yes, hmmm, technically a <u>doctor</u>," said the pompous old fool.

"It was nothing, John, just a brief…"

"Peccadillos happen, Candice."

"I'm sorry I told you, John. Let's just forget…"

"No, we're both adults, Candy. Let's talk about it."

"Later perhaps. Someone has to see to our patients."

"Yes, and I am a…a taller <u>medical</u> doctor," said her husband, putting on his starched white jacket. "Bring in the first victim," he said, putting on a rubber glove, "along with a healthy dose of *Mister Bones*."

CHAPTER FIFTEEN

With the kid out of school and now back to sitting across from him, eagerly listening and learning as he jotted, Max again leaned back in his double-wide chair and again put his feet on the desk, prepared to conclude a slightly revised account of *Case of Dickwork Outside the Box,* but...

"Are you saying that, uh, 'remains' of Doc Sanders' Missus and the hairdresser are in that box?" said the kid. "Are you saying the doc murrrderrred them in a fit of jealousy, and put the box here on the desk to avenge...what, your meddling in his marital relations and/or telling him the awful truth?"

"Not even close to the awful truth," said Max. The old doc was the *femme fatale's* lap dog, he explained. Wouldn't dare nip off an ear of his Missus.

"Oh," said the kid, putting his pencil behind his own stuck-out ear. "So no murrrderrr to be jotted about?"

"Wake up and smell the sausage, kid. The cougar obviously had the doc cut off the hairdresser's ears, put 'em in the box and bring 'em to Yours Truly as payback for..."

"For putting the doc wise to the hanky-panky going on between her and the hairdresser! Gee, Mr. Max..."

He wanted to be patient with the kid, to whom Yours Truly was an heroic role model, but . .

"...I hope you did the right thing by, uh, meddling."

With a sigh, Max realized he would have to spell out the facts of life by chapter-and-verse for the green-as-Saint Patrick's Day-beer case report jotter.

The man-eating cougar's beef was not that Yours Truly had

"meddled", he explained. The doc's Missus—like the sister's jealous, brutish husband in Holmes' *Case of the Cardboard Box*—had her underwear in a wad because Yours Truly gave the cold shoulder to her advances in the medical exam room.

"But why have the doc cut off...?"

"Listen and learn, kid. It was a set-up."

"A set-up?"

Max patiently explained that the *femme fatale* must have seen through his disguise at the tea room, and—with a frame-up in mind—lured him to follow her to the beauty parlor in Okmulgee. No doubt a camera behind the parlor door's peep-hole was used to place—and incriminate—Yours Truly at what was to be a bloody crime scene.

"Made the mistake of not donning my usual disguise," he admitted.

"The plastic nose attached to the eyeglass frames and black mustache?"

"Yeah, didn't want to risk dangling another male victim in the cougar's path."

"Hmmm," the kid hmmmed, giving the cardboard box another once-over, then...

"How did you dope out that the, uh, partial 'remains' are those of the hairdresser, Mr. Max? Sunburn, for instance, would not necessarily mean..."

"Didn't bother to look," Max admitted. "Put two-and-two together," he explained, without also irrelevantly admitting that the sight of even dried blood made his heart flutter, his knees weak, his head...

"We'd better check before wrapping up the case report," said the kid, up on his feet and, uh oh, opening the box.

"Hmmm," the young wannabe P.I. then again hmmmed, peering into the cardboard container, and..."Nothing in here except what look to be documents of some kind."

Documents?

Max, up on his own feet, looked into the opened box and... sure enough, detected Yours Truly's old medical records. Eyeing

the top doc—Notary Public lingo for document...

PHYSICAL EXAM SUMMARY

Date: 12/ 05 /2010

PATIENT NAME: Maxwell Morgan **ID:** 203399674

GENDER: Male

RACE: White

BIRTH DATE: 03/ 16 /1974 **AGE:** 37 **Yrs.**9 **Mos.**

HEIGHT: 5 **Ft.** 10 **In.** **WEIGHT:** 238 **Pounds**

Max scanned a list of boxes headlined **BIOMARKERS**...

[X] High LDL

[X] Low HDL

[X] High Triglycerides

[X] High Hypertension

[X] High BUN

[X] High AST

   ...then skipped to:

COMMENTS

Sedentary Lifestyle...Poor Diet...Excessive Sleepiness... Morbid Obesity.

Hmmm. Looked not too bad, but...Scribbled at the bottom of the page in what must have been Doc Sanders' handwriting:

Patient's remaining life expectancy: 15 to 20 years.

Max did the math inside his head, and...Oh no, immediately he noticed fluttering chest pains. Urine ran down his leg onto the copy shop cubicle floor. Inside his head...bright white light.

THE

END